AFTER IT HAPPENED

BOOK 6: REBELLION

DEVON C FORD

VULPINE
P R E S S

Published by Vulpine Press in the United Kingdom in 2017

Cover by Claire Townsend

ISBN: 978-1-83919-239-5

www.vulpine-press.com

PROLOGUE

"Is it tonight?" Jan asked Steve excitedly, nervous apprehension twisting his insides. The older man thought for a moment before answering him.

"Yes," Steve answered simply. "I'll signal the start; everyone should know what they have to do, and if they don't, well then it's just too late to change it now."

Jan nodded and turned to leave the room but swung back to face Steve when he heard his name called.

"Don't die," Steve said to him seriously before grabbing him close for a rough hug of solidarity. It was more than that, though. The two men had been thrown together by chance and had become not only close friends, but brothers. Comrades. The instigators of a rebellion which would, tonight, one way or another, change the lives of everyone in their camp forever. Jan hugged him back, patting his back roughly with a big hand, and assured the pilot that he wouldn't die.

"I mean it," Steve added vehemently before pulling away and cracking a small smile. "Otherwise I'd have to find someone else dumb enough to get punched in the head as much as you do."

Looking back and responding with a crude but good-natured insult in his native Afrikaans, he turned once more and left the room. Tonight he would fight, only this time he would fight to the best of his abilities. He would not test the waters, or play the crowd, or lose intentionally to an opponent so as to pick and choose who he fights next. Tonight he would put any man who wanted to stop him in the ground, and only when he faced the best warriors this place could serve up to him would they truly see what he could do. Relishing the prospect of facing either of the brothers, Will or Benjamin, in the arena without his own self-imposed limitations, he vowed to show them the cost of taking him for a fool.

Tonight, he thought to himself, *shit or bust, I'm going to unleash hell.* If he died, he died. He chuckled to himself at the film reference before his face dropped into seriousness as he began to flex and stretch his muscles. Walking towards the pit where the underground fighting took place made his heart rate increase and his breathing became more rapid. This would be the fifth time he had stepped into the arena; the four occasions before had left him with a week or two of physical recovery from the beatings he had received. *Intentionally received*, he reminded himself. *Tonight would be different*, he thought with a cruel smile tickling the corners of his mouth as he waited in the dark, metal container for his turn to fight. Winner stays on, and tonight he would be staying on until the very end.

Peeling off his shirt and going into the arena bare-chested for the first time, he heard noises as people finally saw how honed his body was; he hid his strength and size behind a happy and jovial personality, but there was no humour in him tonight.

Eying up his opponent he decided that round one of the Jan show would take a matter of seconds. He would tease and purposefully displease the crowd like that with a few opponents; dropping them quickly and offering no entertainment. That would get the crowd baying for a stronger fighter to join in and he hoped to meet the resident champion, Will.

When he or his brother stepped onto the hard ground inside the arena with Jan, they would die. Jan was about to cause the mother of all distractions.

And then the rebellion would begin.

BORING AS HELL

Alice absent-mindedly wiped an infected cut with antiseptic fluid, causing her patient to flinch and gasp at the stinging sensation. She didn't care much for their discomfort; the injuries were self-inflicted in her opinion. Ignorance was as much to blame for the infection as the injury itself.

Not that she was ever asked for her opinion. She was part of the machine: a small cog in a great contraption which ran on human beings. Get up, go to work fixing people who were broken, eat, sleep, repeat.

Her life since the invasion of their home was one of repetition, boredom, and wistful dreaming of another way to exist. She had considered a way out of that existence more than once. She had even been fortunate enough to find the medicine cabinet unlocked and was seconds away from self-administering a fatal dose of morphine when she came to her senses. It was only the small glimmer of hope which made her carry on with her dull life. The hope that Steve could somehow overthrow Richards, subdue his small army and take control of the camp.

It wasn't like their old home. This place was vast; almost a thousand people at her best guess, not that she was trusted to see any documentation or records. She was just a lowly nurse who treated injuries caused by stupidity and illnesses which any ten-year-old with a library book could diagnose.

It was bizarre, she thought, that she could barely recall her life before the world fell apart. She was away at university when it happened, studying for her degree in mathematics. Studying was perhaps a little strong; she was out four nights a week doing what any self-respecting student would do and making poor life choices whilst under the influence of very cheap alcohol. Now she was a nurse, and in some ways she had been a nurse her whole life; if her whole life qualified as the year since Dan had saved her from two savages with machetes and a loose understanding of the law surrounding sexual consent.

Her father, Mike, had been badly hurt and still bore the horrific scars from the cuts which would surely have killed him if it weren't for their rescue. Kate, a paramedic, had saved his life and later spent all her spare time teaching Alice the basics of emergency medicine. Lizzie had joined their small medical team too. It was a blessing that she was still there with her, even if they were forced to work differing shifts and barely had a chance to speak to one another. Lizzie had always been kind and motherly to her.

As she wiped roughly at the affected area and prompted more pained noises, her consciousness returned to the present. The wound, as small as it was, would need antibiotics if the infection was to be stopped before it poisoned the body. The thought of their finite supply of antibiotics stung at the edges of her consciousness for a second until she pushed it away. She had learned to concentrate only on the things she could immediately influence otherwise the stress would eat her up.

"Go and wait over there,' she told the patient without looking at him. "You'll need to see the doctor."

Making a few notes in the patient's file and placing it at the bottom of the in tray, which served as a waiting list, the injured man shuffled off to wait for his turn to be prescribed a course of medication which simple hygiene could have negated.

Returning to clean up her work station, her mind wandered again back to their former life at the prison. A quick mental inventory made for depressing reading: Dan was gone, having taken Kate, Marie, Leah and more than a dozen other people to chase some dream in Africa. The dream was that they could find some miracle cure for whatever caused women to have stillborn babies - ironic, as there was a newborn baby at their own camp which had all of the medical staff scratching their heads. After they had gone, newcomers had arrived at their home and not long after, they had betrayed them and brought in Richards's entire army. They were all swept up, catalogued, bundled into trucks and set to work in the new camp. They were prisoners, but they were fed and protected. If freedom was starvation and fear, then captivity had to have some benefits she thought.

She often wondered what happened to the others. She saw people every day that she used to live with. She slept in her allocated cot in a room with no less than three of her former housemates. She saw Lizzie most days on shift change and she had even seen Steve once, when fate conspired to put them in the same room. That was a shock to her, as she had only learned the day before, by overhearing gossip, that he was still alive. Alice and Lizzie had tried so hard to keep him stable after he barely survived a helicopter crash. Lizzie had reset the bones of his lower leg but the internal injuries were beyond what equipment and training they had to be able to fix him. By the time he finally awoke from a coma, it was too late; the invading forces had come for them.

She knew her father still lived, that knowledge had found her shortly after arriving at the new camp. She had been treating a man with a twisted ankle when he whispered to her.

"Are you Alice?" he said softly so as not to attract the attention of the ever-present armed guards.

"Yes," she replied, not taking her eyes off her task.

"Mike's alive. He wanted you to know that he loves you," said the man with a smile of achievement and happiness. Fighting down an emotional sob of elation, Alice picked up the man's file and carefully read how the injury had happened from the triage nurse's notes. He worked as part of an engineering party tasked with manufacturing and repairing farming tools. That made sense, she thought, her father was an engineer after all. Her elation at the news was short-lived, as there was no way of seeing him unless he ended up in the medical wing.

Still, he was alive.

She was alive, and that was really all she could ask for.

Shaking herself out of her reverie, she looked at the growing line of the sick and injured.

"Next," she called in a bored monotone.

THEY SEE WHAT THEY WANT TO SEE

Steve was happy, in some small way. He had a purpose, and as he recalled Dan saying many times, people loved a purpose. It gave them a reason to get up, a reason not to give up, and motivated even the laziest of people to think about the future.

His version of the future haunted him day and night. His vision of standing on top of the steps to the camp headquarters and looking out over a massed crowd of frightened people; his vision of Richards dead at his feet; his vision of the elite guard killed in simultaneous actions all orchestrated by the whispers and rumours of the underground. Half of that network already existed, human nature dictates a need for gossip, but he needed to organise it. He needed to give the gossip a purpose; to steel it towards action, to gather the intelligence and form a plan ready to execute when the time was right.

He was certain that it wouldn't take much. Most of the guards were guards simply because it offered an easier, more privileged life. *The path of least resistance*, Dan had called it. The guards watched people and reported what they said in return for avoiding the manual labour. There was very little in the way of overt lawlessness, and credit where it was due, Richards ran a relatively tidy ship. That wasn't to say that bad things didn't happen, and he made a horrific example of one of his soldiers who had sexually assaulted a woman in camp.

Hundreds of people were rounded up and ordered into the large square outside headquarters. Richards took a microphone and peevishly explained the man's crime, the disgust in his voice clearly evident. After the explanation, with no mention of having established the man's guilt - not that it mattered, it seemed - he was summarily executed by firing squad.

No more rumours of guards mistreating residents reached Steve's ears, but the oppression was far from over.

Now, having been finally allowed to rejoin the general population after his recovery had been mostly endured in solitude, he shuffled around leaning heavily on a walking stick and seeming, to all the world who cared, to look like a broken man. He was a shadow of his former self; a man who had flown helicopters in all weathers day and night in war-zones, and had even defied Richards by breaking his word and stealing a helicopter from him last year. Ironically, that same helicopter was the one that he had almost died in and still sat, mangled and rusting, next to the ornate building they used to call home.

He was happy that people saw him as an invisible, old cripple. They didn't know the truth.

The truth was, despite the life-threatening injuries he had received a few months ago, he was actually in good health. The limp was real due to the catastrophic break it had suffered, but he pronounced it to such a degree that nobody could tell at a glance that he would be able to drop the stick and sprint at any moment. He wore his clothes loose and oversized intentionally to make him appear thin and weak, when in fact he exercised feverishly when alone. He was as fit as the day he had lost control of the tail rotor of his Merlin and fought to keep it level as he ploughed into the soft, green earth so many weeks ago.

His physical state wasn't the only ruse he was proud of. Richards had summoned him on three occasions since he regained his health, and on all three meetings Steve had been assured of Richards's insanity. He was also impressed that it was so effectively veiled behind logical planning and, he had to admit, a degree of efficiency in how the camp was run. He had fooled Richards into believing that he only wanted some company and a simple life for his dwindling days, and Richards's arrogance made that lie believable. He had been given a menial job in the kitchens and allocated sleeping space with other people. Both concessions allowed him an unprecedented level of interaction with others, and from there served him well in forming the secret network of gossips into an ordered rebellion. He recruited lieutenants who knew the identities of other members and held trusted information, and slowly the network grew organically. He had nothing else to think about, and it became an obsession which filled every waking moment. One thing he was sure to do was insulate one member of the rebellion from another; if a person was interrogated or tortured for information - which was likely given Richards's degree of paranoia - then they could only give up one or two people before they simply knew nothing of the others involved. Each layer had another layer, and that insulation protected him a hundred times over.

Over a few months he had made subtle contact with many of his former group members and learned that more than a few were unaccounted for.

In order to further the level of insulation, he carefully planned a break of anonymity in the low of information by way of using dead-drops, whereby a lower level informant would leave information at a set place during a time of high activity and would never know who picked it up and passed it on.

The only missing man whose fate was known was Ewan, their fiery Welsh farmer. Never one to be accused of having an introverted personality, he had refused to accept his place in the new order and ended up taking one severe beating too many. He died within a week of being brought to the camp and forced to tend livestock. The incident which led to his death was initially a simple misunderstanding, but when Ewan tried to explain something to people he had a tendency to come across as more than a little aggressive. That aggression had been reciprocated, and like two cockerels puffing up their chests the testosterone had become too great a force to be resisted. Ewan had died, and everyone else went back to work.

That was just one of a thousand injustices for which Richards would burn, Steve promised himself.

If he allowed himself to grieve for his losses, to lament over the things he regretted, then it was Leah he missed the most. The young girl he had spent twelve hours a day training to use weapons, the girl who had become formidable and frightening, but was still the same sweet girl who viewed everything in a positive and simplistic way, taking each day as it came. Returning to his menial task of wiping clean and stacking the plastic trays ready for another meal serving, he wondered what she was doing and where she was.

LIFE INSIDE THE WALL

It had been weeks since they had found themselves safe behind the impregnable walls of Sanctuary, but Leah still felt half dressed. After the initial shock of finding safety, and the bigger shock of discovering that their onward journey was no longer necessary, she had finally realised something very important.

Having worn the same ballistic vest for as long as she could remember without it being washed, it stank.

That had been the first time she hadn't either slept in the thickly padded Kevlar or at least donned it the second she woke up.

Now, wrapped warmly against the bitter winter winds coming straight from the sea to her position high on the ramparts, she still felt strange not having the extra weight of body armour. Her feet felt light, like she was walking around in reduced gravity, and she began to suspect that her need to wear the vest was possibly more psychological than practical.

Even though they were technically disarmed when they had entered Sanctuary, Leah was still carrying two knives and had squirrelled a suppressed handgun into her clothes when they moved into their comfortable new quarters.

Still, she felt almost unnatural not waking before the dawn to watch for attacks. The relaxed atmosphere and the utter belief in their safety inside Sanctuary stuck in her throat too. It felt totally alien to not post sentries, other than one person being on duty to open and close the gate when required, and that person appearing to be as useful in a fight as coffee cup made of ice. In her opinion, they were just asking for trouble.

But that was the thing here; she was just a child, a female one at that, and nobody asked for her opinion about the important things.

Of all the things she found strange being inside a safe enclave, it was the fact that others looked at her like a child again. Everyone who knew her would likely bet good money on her in a fight with most people, but everyone in Sanctuary wanted to treat her like a kid again.

She wasn't unhappy - far from it - but after the months of adrenaline and feeling like everyone needed her, she was bored. She had nothing to stimulate her brain. She didn't want to fish or play or do normal people jobs: she was a warrior, albeit an unorthodox one, and she craved the chance to do what she was trained for.

Dan was no help in that respect. He had wholly embraced their new lifestyle of comfort and safety and was completely obsessed with Marie's ever-swelling belly. Leah knew that he should be, but he could at least pretend to agree with her that they should be allowed their weapons back. She was genuinely happy for them, and for herself too, but it stung a little that someone who wasn't even born yet took all the attention already. She remembered a time not too long before when Dan's obsession was on the survival and protection of their group.

Feeling lost as she looked out over the ancient, high walls of the huge central keep, gazing out at a fishing boat struggling back into the protected bay against the choppy winter sea, her attention was pulled back to her only companion.

A loud yawn followed by a curious dance as Ash sought the perfect position to scratch his ear with his back foot brought a smile to her face.

"You bored too, boy?" she asked him. Ash answered her with a sudden stare until he let out a sneeze and shook his head in surprise at the confusion it caused him. A scratch of boot on stone made her turn sharply, ever alert, and reach instinctively for the worn hilt of the knife hidden in the back of her waistband. Framed in the archway at the top of a flight of stone steps stood an equally bored Mitch. He had been soldiering his whole life and the two shared a strange kindred spirit. They were equally unimpressed at being caged without even being allowed to organise adequate defences.

The subject had been raised to Polly, the curious and vague French-Canadian woman who seemed to run this place when she wasn't talking to herself. It had been summarily dismissed, but it was clear that the occupants of Sanctuary had not seen anywhere near their fair share of modern life. They had not been attacked, they had accepted anyone who turned up into their home and left it almost entirely undefended.

That wasn't strictly true, Leah allowed. The geography of this half natural, half man-made place was defence enough against all but the most determined and experienced attacker. However, that didn't stop her mind working overtime every morning when she came up to the highest central point to survey the whole bay and plan the defences she wished she could implement. It wasn't about being hostile towards others, not in her head at least, it was about not being a fool because there were plenty of people out there who had proven they would kill for even the most meagre stash of food. Sighing at the exhausting uselessness of arguing against the majority, she shot a sad smile at Mitch.

"Here again?" he asked her to fill the silence.

"Yeah," she said, conveying every frustrating ounce of boredom she felt bearing down on her young shoulders and old soul.

"What's on your mind?" he asked her, knowing the probable answer but interested to hear her articulate it.

Taking a deep breath and gathering her thoughts, she pointed to the gatehouse. "Twin machine guns on the gate, interlocking arcs of fire to smother the approach road." Mitch nodded at the obvious suggestion. Pointing her other hand to the sky fort high above the road she continued, "Heavy gun up there trained on the road. Something a bit heavier if we can find it, explosives or something, snipers too, to cut off any retreat."

"Not bad," he responded, "what about a seaward attack?"

Turning to face the water she pointed to the watchtower firstly on the low sea wall, then to the one high on the cliff in the distance. "Crew-served gun there; it'll cut any boat to shreds. Distance might be a bit much for another one on the cliff, and a slightly wrong angle would hit the other gun position. Sniper *there*," she said, squinting along her outstretched finger pointed at the tower on the high cliff opposite. "But their position is more tactical than defensive as it offers a full view of the valley; they will be our first warning of any attack."

Impressed, Mitch agreed.

"Do you know who's up there?" he asked.

"One old man from what I heard. That needs to change as it needs twenty-four hour cover. And some kind of comms system," she finished, her sadness at feeling useless crushing her spirit once more.

"Cheer up," Mitch told her, still smiling and changing the subject. "I've bagged us a trip outside the walls!"

Elated, the old Leah returned instantly. Her stance grew taller and more confident, prompting Ash to smarten himself up as though he sensed it was time to go to work.

Shrugging into her shabby vest after a hasty change of clothes, Leah tightened the Velcro sides and settled her equipment to make it more comfortable. Feeling the recurring stab of annoyance that she had to have her weapons issued to her by someone who didn't have the first clue how to use them, she waited patiently at the inner gate as Mitch explained where they were going.

"Supply run to one of the farms," he told her. "They haven't got much to harvest this time of year, so the flow of supplies reverses now. Just some basics, but there are nearly fifty people relying on us outside of the walls."

Mitch had gleaned this kind of information as his own boredom had led him not to stare outwards wistfully, but to talk to everyone so that he could and learn the comings and goings of Sanctuary. He had casually suggested his offer of additional security, blaming their arrival as the cause for possible hostilities, and had made himself a sufficient nuisance to be given permission to tag along with a basic supply run.

In his inactivity, Mitch had learned a lot about their new home. The impossibly high walls between the two cliff faces protected a large bay, which in turn was protected on the seaward side by two other cliffs, one very high and the other little more than a sea wall culminating in a watch tower. The peaks surrounding them provided a stream which ran through the town and into the calm bay where fishing boats went out daily to bring in a new catch. The supply of fresh fish was eternal, and didn't rely on the weather to be so bountiful in contrast to one of the two farms they were visiting that day.

What had become quickly apparent was that Sanctuary itself wasn't the only place for survivors; it was the central hub. The safe place where the region's inhabitants contracted to if threatened. It was a walled burgh like in feudal Britain where farmers brought their livestock when the Vikings landed on their nearby shores, and waited in safety until the threat went away. It was the main warren for a lot of rabbits, and one of the other burrows was their target now. From what he had gathered, there were two farms each about twenty miles inland. There was also the watch tower high on the far cliff overlooking their calm bay and no means to get to it other than to climb a steep track. There was also a camp set against the two huge wind turbines where a small team of engineers and their young apprentices stayed, making their daily checks of the machinery and teaching everything they knew to the next generation. The only other associated settlement was the sky fortress which overlooked the road to Sanctuary's main gateway. Covering the only approach from a sickeningly high vantage point, the fort was accessible only one of two ways; by air, which was an unlikely option unless you had evolved to grow wings, or by the seven hundred stone steps cut out of the very heart of the mountains centuries ago. This tunnel led directly back to the guard post near the main gate, and resupplying the few lookouts who lived there had become very labour intensive. So much so, that they had ingeniously rigged a high-tensile cable between the main keep and the fort and operated a manual pulley system to bring up a large wicker basket of food daily. He had yet to summon the energy to visit the fort, and didn't look forward to the almost half a kilometre climb via the very long staircase.

All of these facts were filed neatly in his brain until such time as his fellow soldiers required a report, at which point he would succinctly recite everything he had learned. Until then, he was just glad for the fresh air and a small sense of purpose for his teenaged-ninja friend. As he settled his weapons and chambered a round, he looked at Leah to see her doing the same. She had regained the look he had become accustomed to; a look of watchful apprehension where he knew she could spring into action at a moment's notice. His ribs and chest were still sore from the bullet which had slammed into his vest weeks ago, but the memory of his near-death did nothing to dissuade his need to be outside taking the fight to any enemy foolish enough to test the mettle of a British soldier.

Ash was at Leah's side, and he doubted whether she had found the time to ask Dan's permission to take the dog. *Not that it matters*, he thought, Dan had gone into some kind of social coma since they had arrived there and spent most of his time talking to Polly or the strange man who stayed in the highest tower of the keep. Mitch hadn't ventured into the social circle of French post-apocalyptic living much, other than to smile at a pretty woman who he had seen around the town more than a few times.

Loaded and ready, they fell in watchful step beside a horse-drawn cart as it began its ponderous journey inland.

L'ENCYCLOPÉDIE

"I don't see how it's possible though," interrupted Dan for the third time.

Victor made a sympathetic face and tried to figure another way to form the sentence that the primitive Dan could more easily understand. At least he thought the face he made was sympathetic, almost everyone else thought it made him look smug and superior.

Victor was a professor of history who had found himself, for the first time, totally alone when disaster struck the human race. He had known where to go and what to bring, having spent some time during his doctorate discussing this very scenario, give or take a few minor variations, as a thought experiment for a future thesis paper. He was an expert in many fields. He held degrees which he had earned in Paris, in England and even attended Harvard on a scholarship. His research and work had taken him to every continent in the world and his knowledge was vast.

For all his intellect, though, he had never made a true friend and had never been physically tested until the day he found himself totally alone.

That said, his vast knowledge and high intellect stood for precisely nothing the first time he tried to actually do any number of things he felt over-qualified for, without the support network of a functioning society.

Opening his eyes and fixing Dan with a look, he tried one last time.

"As your friend Emma has explained to you, twice now in fact, the subject is quite simple. There are many things we cannot explain as we do not yet have the capability to test our theories and prove them as fact. But the best minds surviving the event," meaning himself, "have agreed that, given what we know, this is our best working theory."

His English was flawless and only barely accented, which Dan guessed was a product of having lived and studied in English speaking countries for years. Still, the man's manner irked him and he didn't enjoy being spoken to like a child. Shooting a glance at Emma for backup, she tried to tell him again.

"From what we know," she said in her small, nervous voice before clearing her throat and starting again, louder this time. "From what we know, some form of prehistoric pathogen was released by the science experiment and that rapidly became airborne and infected everyone on the planet. Some of us, obviously, are immune and the only thing we have in common is that all of us have undergone treatment involving anti-malarial drugs."

"I get that," Dan said with feigned patience. "I'm asking about the fact that some people can have babies and others can't."

"Everyone can have babies," said Victor, "at least those physically capable anyway. It's just that our immunity has led to certain side effects."

"Exactly," said Emma, taking up the explanation again. "Whatever makes us immune can only be a mutation - like an evolutionary mutation: something so small as to never be noticeable unless something like, well, this, happens. Whatever makes us immune to the pathogen is rendered harmless by the mutation which, we're guessing, was caused by our individual exposure to the drugs we were given. That mutation has to be in our blood because that is the cause of death for the foetus and mother in childbirth."

Seeing Dan's face drop to a look of cold hostility made her change her tone rapidly as she recalled he was hoping to be a father soon. "What I mean is," she went on hurriedly, "that because they figured out what the problem was, they figured out a fix: during pregnancy our blood will thicken because of the mutation which makes us able to still be alive. That is both our cure and our curse because surviving the event is pointless unless the species can propagate."

"You're rambling," Dan said quietly. Emma swallowed. He had clearly had his fill of science and wanted it put simply for him.

"Blood thinners, like Warfarin, given to pregnant women make having babies possible."

"OK," said Marie, who until then had sat in still silence behind her frustrated man. "So I have Warfarin and our baby will be born alive?"

Victor and Emma glanced at one another briefly.

"Yes," they both said at once.

"There you go then," she said, patting Dan's leg and climbing to her feet. "Problem solved."

Dan sat with his mouth open, wanting to know more about everything and feeling let down that Marie was happy to leave given the easiest of explanations.

Emma stood and walked out with her, leaving Dan to follow up in frustrated confusion.

"Dan, if you will, please?" said Victor behind him.

Turning, he saw the man gesturing to a chair. Clearly the professor wanted more from him. With a frustrated noise of resignation, he gave up on following the annoyingly satisfied Marie and sat heavily.

"Pointless," Dan muttered to himself, prompting Victor's eyebrows to raise in question.

"Africa. Crossing the Channel. Leaving home. All of it was bloody pointless when we could've figured this out anywhere," he said, sounding more annoyed with himself than anything else.

"Life is about the journey, not the destination," Victor said magnanimously as he eyed Dan.

Dan wasn't in the mood for inspirational quotes, even if he suspected that articular one was a song lyric, and said nothing.

Rising from his own chair with a resigned sigh, Victor poured two glasses of the curious local liquor and handed Dan one as he sat down again.

"Do you know what the original encyclopaedia was?" he asked, changing the subject.

Dan sipped, and then fell back to sullen flippancy as his default setting.

"Was it the thing I used to copy my homework from?"

Victor smiled at the poor joke and deflected causally. "No, Dan. In 1751 Denis Diderot - a famous French philosopher - published the first volume of *L'Encyclopédie*. He intended it to be a safe repository of the knowledge of all mankind, if you like a time capsule for future generations in case the learning history of our species was eradicated. I believe that this is what has happened to us, no? Our world was dependent on fossil fuels, on the great power plants that supplied whole cities with power, and every person alive had the capacity to access any piece of knowledge they needed. Terrorists need to make a bomb? They learn how to do so on the internet. You need to know how to replace a part on your car? Look on the internet and follow a video guide showing you each and every step. The encyclopaedia was designed as just this; not just the knowledge of man but the means to replicate it. Do you understand?" He looked at Dan, his enthusiasm unveiled as though he were giving a lecture to just one man instead of a room of university graduates.

"Yeah," said Dan, "it was an instruction manual for what we already know how to do."

"Exactly this! So tell me, do you know how to make the weapons you are so skilled at using?"

Dan was annoyed at the theatricality of the question. Obviously he hadn't the first clue how to manufacture an automatic weapon, so he stayed silent assuming that the question was rhetorical.

"Of course you don't!" Victor went on, proving Dan right again. "But do you know how to use it? Do you have, tucked deep inside your mind, the knowledge of how to show others the best way to use it?"

His thoughts drifted to Leah. To Lexi. To all the others he had taught how to shed their previous lives and become soldiers of necessity.

"Yes," he replied simply.

"So if I collect your intricate knowledge of this, and combine it with the knowledge from elsewhere of how to make these weapons, then future generations can continue to use technology that is beyond their scope to discover. Do you see this, Dan?"

"Yes," he replied again, "you want to get the skills that everyone has written down in your books so we don't lose any technology for future generations."

Victor was pleased that this simple, yet frighteningly scarred man had grasped his concept so quickly. Beckoning the man he suspected to be a barely-evolved Neanderthal to the other side of his chambers, he presented a large book which bore Victor's neat script on the open pages.

"And that is what I hope to do here, so I would greatly appreciate some of your time when I am available to pluck the knowledge from your mind and record it in my books."

Dan stood, no longer willing to play along.

"No problem," he said, draining his glass before heading for the door.

Stepping out onto the high stone walkways as he lit a cigarette from the unfamiliar packet having resupplied with more French tobacco, he enjoyed a solitary stroll along the ancient battlements to gather his thoughts. Glancing down at the approach road, he recognised two shapes from the procession heading uphill.

"Where the hell is she going with my dog?" he asked himself aloud.

THE SAFETY BUBBLE

As Dan wandered back along the exposed walkways in search of anything constructive to do, he almost collided with Polly who was scurrying along with armfuls of rolled paper.

She had reluctantly told them that her previous life was spent as an architect who specialised in open-air projects; parks and the like. Her experience and understanding of architectural history made her choice of places to seek safety in very limited. Limited to one, in fact, which is exactly where she ended up within days of the world taking a hard right into terrifying.

She had been visiting an old college friend in southern Spain when it hit, and she immediately packed her few belongings and drove the rental car over the mountains to seek safety. In her panic she drove the small car off the road when distracted, forcing her to walk the last thirty miles to the town with dried blood on her face from the cut on her scalp.

What she found surprised her, shocked her in fact. She found only a few people milling around in confused terror without the first idea how to start rebuilding their lives. Polly knew that they had weeks, maybe months, of relatively easy living without proper organisation and that was where her natural ability and experience shone through. Having spent most of her adult life in and around the construction industry, she had found herself alone in her gender on most days. She had adapted well to this, and quickly showed a flair for managing the rough men under the control of her project management. Often they tried to intimidate her just for fun with crude jokes and unsavoury conversations, only to realise, to their embarrassment, that she could out-crude their own humour, and could do it so quickly and publicly that her reputation grew as a woman not to mess with.

People who knew her joked that she carried such a large handbag around because she needed the extra space for all the balls she had removed from the men working for her.

But that was a lifetime ago.

What had happened to the world had rocked Polly. Rocked her so much that, unknowingly, she had tipped over. She had always been an anxious person before, though to look at her you would only see a fiercely organised woman who has no time for procrastination; look a little closer and you would see her eyes glaze over sometimes as she became momentarily unaware of the world outside of her head. She was often seen talking to herself, arguing even, but she pushed away any further speculation by smiling back and informing them that she had to speak to herself in order to get a sensible answer.

Dan saw it. Dan suspected that it indicated something far deeper than peculiar habits, not that he judged her on her flaws; god knew he was probably one dropped plate away from a screaming breakdown most days.

Dan's concerns were natural. Instinctive. Ingrained. So deeply rooted in his psyche that if you snapped him open the words *suspicious bastard* would be found running through his whole body like a stick of hard candy.

"Sorry," he muttered to the tutting woman who was on her hands and knees retrieving the scattered architectural sketches. He bent to help only to have the one roll of paper he had retrieved snatched from his grasp rudely.

Seeing the look of shock on Dan's face, Polly reset her manner by closing her eyes and opening them to start again. When she opened them, Dan was startled to see such a different look in her eyes that she could have been a different person.

"No, I'm sorry," she said in her peculiar accent; a mixture of Canadian and French that was so unique Dan had still not grown used to the sound of her voice. "I wanted to…"

She stopped, her eyes focusing on the lit cigarette in his hand. Reading this distraction completely wrong, Dan reached for his pack to offer her one.

"Oh! No thank you!" she said flustered. "I never smoked… cigarettes anyway," she finished in a quieter tone. A wry smile pickled the left side of Dan's mouth, making the ugly scar running down the left side of his face crease and transform him from brooding to amused.

"Well I haven't got any of that, sorry," he said, still smiling.

"No, I wasn't suggesting… sorry!" Polly stammered, embarrassed that she had told a secret to a stranger.

"OK," Dan went on, changing the subject. "Let's just stop apologising to each other, shall we?"

"Yes. Sorry," Polly answered, straightening herself. "How can I help you?" she asked.

Dan's confusion was momentary before he recovered and told her that he didn't almost knock her over on purpose to get her attention.

Embarrassed again, Polly remembered that it was actually she who was on the lookout for him and not the other way around.

Deciding on the aloof recovery method, she capitalised on the chance encounter.

"Well seeing as I bumped into you, no pun intended, I wonder would you walk with me a minute?"

Dan fell into step alongside her as she went at a slower pace along the windy, exposed stone walkways. Polly fell back on facts to fill the time and ignore the biting cold cutting through her clothes. "These walls have never been breached," she said suddenly, nodding over the ramparts to the approach road. "The town has been besieged so many times throughout history, even before the fortifications and the defences - impregnable at the time. The Spanish kept trying to take the town claiming it was theirs. It's been traded between countries, even betrayed once, but never beaten."

Dan nodded in silence, suspecting that the subject he was waiting for was about to be raised.

"I've been thinking for a while now, even before you arrived, that we haven't seen the kind of behaviour you would expect; no violence or looting. Maybe we are too isolated?" she said. Dan stayed silent, knowing that the safe cocoon that enveloped the town was burst when he and his gang arrived.

"How would you attack this town?" she asked him almost casually, as though the answer mattered only as conversation.

Expecting this to come sooner or later, Dan took a breath and attempted to annoy the woman slightly in order that his real suggestion be listened to. "Four-man team would come in from the bay using scuba gear under cover of darkness. Just before dawn I'd have a high-altitude-high-opening parachute team of two snipers take out the watch tower on the cliffs and both teams would start picking off the sentries on the fort silently. Garrison the gatehouse, use mortar rounds or drone strikes to suppress the fort then take it via the stairs. Obviously having a satellite overhead giving us infrared coverage and a command and control room to advise us via radio too," he said, deliberately making his plan sound like an action movie. Turning to face Polly with a smile to meet her frown, he waited to be berated. Instead she closed her eyes momentarily, opening them again and asking a more specific question to negate the flippancy of his last answer.

"If you were to try and take this town, from an outsider's point of view, given today's *limitations*, then how would you go about it?"

Dan thought for a moment. "At the moment," he started, "quite easily." He glanced at her to see that she wasn't the slightest bit shocked. "I'd need twenty fighters, come in by boat and completely overwhelm any defences, of which there are none, then take the gatehouse and then force a surrender from the fort by starving them out or climbing the stairs and killing them. The last option would probably be the only way we would lose any attackers. I'd have probably sent in at least two people a few weeks before with instructions to secure your weapons as soon as the attack started."

Polly sighed. Even before Dan's ragged crew had collapsed on their doorstep, she had suffered sleepless nights about the risk of attack. So far they had seen none of the roving bands of outlaws so associated with an apocalyptic wasteland, but hearing Dan and his group talk about the ambushes and the roadblocks, her concerns had evolved into fears, and those fears were now causing her a significant amount of lost sleep.

"Are you the advance party?" she asked seriously.

"No," Dan replied, mirroring her tone.

"So how do we stop it?" she asked simply.

29

Pausing to lean his back on the stone ledge of the exposed walkway, Dan lit another cigarette from the end of the last one before tossing the stub into the wind.

"I haven't given it much thought," he lied, "but I know someone who has."

DEAD DROP

Steve wiped a damp cloth over each plastic tray, silently counting as he went. At twenty-three he found the small plastic disc he was looking for, quietly swept it into the bin with any other detritus he found left by the diners, and carried on with his task. After the kitchen was cleaned he limped away, leaning heavily on his walking stick as he carried a bag of vegetable peelings, returning the kindly greetings he received from two men walking past.

They pitied him, he could tell. They all pitied him. Even, he suspected those in the resistance who knew who he was. But even those didn't know his full plan or his capabilities. Shrugging away the annoyance of pride for being underestimated, he reminded himself that this was exactly the camouflage he had to maintain. Keeping the number twenty-three securely in his head, he limped on until he found the livestock pens.

To the casual onlooker, this broken man liked to end his working day by taking choice leftovers to the pig pens and smiling as the eager animals snuffled at the treats he brought every evening. Not that any guards were posted to overtly watch him any more, but that wasn't a risk he could afford to take.

On this night, Steve limped alongside the fence, smiling as the most recent piglets squealed with anticipation that it may be their turn to receive an extra ration. Stopping seemingly at random at the twenty-third enclosure, he rested his stick and leaned over the low fence to empty out the bag onto the ground. As the squeaks and snuffles from the mini feeding frenzy below raised the ambient noise level substantially, Steve carefully retrieved the note hidden in the feed bucket attached to the inside of the gate. Keeping it in his hand as he watched the banquet noisily being consumed, he eventually straightened with a satisfied smile. He slipped his free hand containing the note into the pocket of his oversized coat that he wore for warmth against the chill of the winter evening.

Irrelevant to whether he knew or not, Steve was watched from the shadows. Not by the bidding of Richards, for the man in charge had long forgotten about the pilot's treachery and had dismissed him as a threat, but purely by his own volition, Benjamin watched him in secret whenever the chance arose.

Sticking to the shadows he had kept Steve in his sight for over an hour now, and had seen nothing to support his suspicions and feelings of unease about the man. Annoyed, he slipped his black balaclava back over his head and returned to Richards.

~

Safely tucked up in his bed, Steve used his most precious of possessions; a small book light that clipped onto the pages and bathed a small area in bright light to allow him to read in the dark without disturbing others.

Carefully retrieving the note, he laid it smoothly on the page he was reading and, as such, gathered the latest piece of information vital to the efforts of the resistance. His resistance. Not that anyone knew the full extent of his involvement bar a few trusted Lieutenants, and even they didn't have the full picture.

Compartmentalise, insulate, protect.

Gather, watch, listen, wait.

Soon the wait would be over, and the day would come when the cogs in this machine rose to overthrow the tyranny they lived under. Quite what the new world would look like Steve had no idea, but a life where the guards looked outwards instead of inwards had to be better.

Only a few more pieces would need to be placed before he could call checkmate, and he doubted Richards would take the defeat calmly and gently place his king on its side.

They would probably have to wipe the whole board and back him into a corner; and a cornered animal is the most dangerous kind, he told himself.

Shutting off the precious light, he settled down to sleep and plan his next move.

HARD YARDS

Totally bedraggled, Lexi and her companions soldiered onwards. They had not encountered any other people since the primitive ambush attack on them weeks before, but she hadn't taken her eyes from Simon since. The way he turned and seemed to enjoy killing, had disturbed her. So much so that she didn't even know if she had seen it and her mind was playing tricks on her.

They had been forced to rest for a week through a mix of bad weather, low fuel supplies and no food. Finding an abandoned supermarket, they had hidden their vehicle from sight and set up a temporary camp to recoup. Every day they siphoned as much diesel as they could using the handpump and jerrycans until the main tank and the extended range reservoir on the roof were full. Refuelling their bodies was more difficult as, rough as the fuel was becoming, the food supplies had degraded more. Living off canned food, they recovered over that week. When the time came that their exhaustion had faded, and they began to wake feeling relatively refreshed, the reluctant call to continue south was made.

Now deep in mid-France with no sight or smell of the coast, they pushed onwards down the map making slow but steady progress each day, and each day they headed further towards peril.

GREEN CREDENTIALS

It took the lumbering cart three hours to reach the nearest outlying farm from Sanctuary. Leah and Mitch weren't idle on the journey there, both scouting high ground and feeling rejuvenated at getting back to what they did best. Ash bounded along at her side with graceful ease, his quiet paws betraying the fact that he was a killer when called upon.

Mitch watched the girl pause before the skyline so as not to silhouette herself to any enemy. She assessed the ground, eyes darting back and forth between low ground and rocky outcrops. Mitch glanced between the open land ahead and back to the girl beside him. A girl technically, yes, but a warrior at heart and one that people underestimated as their last mistake. He thought to ask her what she was seeing, as he would when training a recruit, but he knew what she would say.

It would be the same as he would say.

"Gulley, six hundred metres ahead, ERV," she would say, meaning that if they suffered an attack and were separated they should head for that scar in the ground and defend it. It would be hard to dig any armed enemy out of there without explosives or air support. Glancing at her again he saw her twist her mouth to the side in concerned thought. He knew what that was about too, and she confirmed his guess by voicing her opinion.

"Mile ahead. Our road hits a pinch-point: steep ground to the left and building to the right. I'd ambush there."

Mitch had seen it already and agreed entirely. If anyone around there had a mind to bring the fight to them, then this place would be a perfect cut off.

It would be the tactics he would use, guerrilla warfare; take out a supply convoy and kill the guards. More trained soldiers would be sent to investigate, and he would lure them into an ambush too. By the time they realised they were under attack they would already have lost a huge percentage of their fighting strength. His mind drifted back to his tours of Northern Ireland a lifetime ago; he had never known stress like it when he had no idea if the person walking down the street minding their own business would turn and shoot him in the back. An enemy stood in formation in front of you was a quantifiable factor; an unseen enemy of mythical number and strength saps the moral from people like an emotional hypothermia.

Bringing himself back to the moment, he agreed by suggesting they scout ahead of the supply wagon.

Jogging forwards at comfortable pace, they abandoned the road to approach from the rear of the building side. That way, if it was set up as an ambush point, they wouldn't be walking into set fields of fire. Assuming the fictional ambushers knew how to organise the most basic of infantry manoeuvres that was.

Carbines up, torches on full, the three of them systematically cleared the first floor of the big building. It was almost immediately apparent that nobody had been inside for months, if not longer, but they carried on with the drill because a good opportunity for a live-fire training exercise should never be wasted. It kept them sharp, and after weeks of relative comfort they had grown a little sluggish in comparison with their usual standards.

At the loud announcement of "Clear", Ash visibly relaxed and returned to pet mode, sitting to scratch at his ear with a hind leg.

Returning to the road, Mitch waved the cart towards them. A mixture of sign language and shouting had made it clear enough that they were to wait until told it was safe. The kindly Frenchman leading his horse humoured the peculiar English, for little other reason than they were an entertaining distraction to an otherwise uneventful life. Besides, such excitement involving guns and soldiers held no interest for him, he just enjoyed seeing others exert unnecessary energy. Clicking his tongue and gently coaxing the placid mare onwards, they resumed their journey for the last mile before the farm.

～

Dropping down from the higher ground of the road, the sprawling expanse of green opened up before Leah's eyes. Sloping higher ground on all sides, the farm sat in a huge natural bowl; an oasis in an otherwise rocky and broken land.

People milled about purposefully but without any urgency. The closer she looked, the more she understood. Dark furrows ran neatly through the greenery where new crops would be planted at the proper time, just like in their own greenhouses back at the prison. Heavy polythene was stretched over wooden frames set low to the ground in protection from the fast winds that blew through the low ground.

As they approached the cluster of single-storey buildings which grew out from the stone-built farmhouse, a small crowd gathered to greet them. A woman wrapped warmly against the bitter wind stepped forward from the group. She had a weathered face and cropped black hair, but she possessed such an air of style and grace that she gave Leah a hint of fierce pride in the woman. Most people saw it as cold, but then again most people lacked a depth of vision.

"You must be the new people," she declared in passable English.

Leah regarded the woman before clicking her fingers to bring Ash to her left heel. He sat obediently at her next subtle hand gesture. Having subconsciously demonstrated that she was no child, she slung her gun and held out a hand to the woman.

"Wow," she answered sarcastically. "What gave us away?" she asked with a smile.

A moment of silence reigned until the woman's stern face cracked into a broad smile and she accepted the outstretched hand.

"I am Nadine," she said.

"Leah," the young girl answered whilst gripping the hand firmly. "Ash and Mitch," she continued, pointing to dog and man in turn.

Despite being relegated in the hierarchy to be behind the dog's social standing, Mitch watched on with a fatherly pride. He had just seen an armed teenage girl totally, yet subtly, dominate a meeting with suspicious foreign allies and disarm their suspicion with the same cocky but capable arrogance that he saw in Dan, which somehow made them both seem endearing.

The apple, he thought to himself, *does not fall far from the tree.*

They were treated to a tour of the simplistic facilities as the supplies were unloaded. They learned from Nadine that twenty of their usual workers had moved to Sanctuary in the winter months to bolster the strength of the small fishing fleet. The majority had remained to tend to the livestock and prepare for the springtime planting boom as well as to fell trees to stockpile logs. Ash bounced alongside them and froze, eyes fixed on something ahead. Leah looked up to see he had locked eyes with another dog, but sensed no threat or malice in eithers body language. "Go on then," she said to him, as though giving a young child permission to run ahead to play. She watched as he bounded up to a dog two thirds his size and the two playfully circled each other before one bolted away, low to the ground, to be chased by the other.

Leah looked at the roof of every one of the low buildings to see small windmills, like children's toys almost, sprouting from each one. Some had two or three.

Seeing her incomprehension, Nadine explained.

"We use the part from the cars. We make our own electricity," she said simply.

Leah frowned and looked to Mitch.

"The alternator," he said. "The bit that charges the car battery from the engine running. I'm guessing you charge batteries from the windmill all day and have lights for the night?" he asked, looking towards their host.

Nadine understood most of what he had said, and nodded.

"We took the batteries from the golf cars," she added.

Smart, Mitch thought, assuming that she meant golf buggies and not the other kind. Car batteries were designed to provide one big blast of power to start an engine, whereas golf buggies were designed to hold charge for longer. With each house having a battery and a couple of micro wind turbines attached, especially with how windy the area was thanks to its geography, they would have a low voltage but near-permanent supply of power.

"Can't believe we never thought of that," Leah said, turning to Mitch.

"Why not? The prison is basically in woodland with very little wind and we had the solar panels, remember?" he answered.

"True," Leah said pensively, realising that she had forgotten a lot of their existence at the prison, which was only a few months ago, as it wasn't relevant to her life right then.

"What about defence?" she asked Nadine, fearing the answer but having to ask anyway.

After a short pause the woman confirmed her worst fears.

"From wolves or people?" she asked.

Ignoring the obvious evasion, Leah glanced at Ash and enquired about the wolves.

"There are packs of wolves that have come down from the mountains now. They come for our animals but we try to keep them away. We have a man who hunts them for us and we have not been troubled by them for many weeks."

Stunned by the information that wild animals were encroaching on human territory out of hunger or outright bravery, Leah fought the spiralling feelings which threatened to take her back to the supply run that almost cost her life. The memory of the pack of wild dogs attacking their routine supply run would stay with her forever, and she had no intention of taking on a wolf pack. Shaking it away, she concentrated on an enemy she was less afraid of.

"And people?" she enquired of Nadine.

"We trust in humanity," she said after a pause, without a hint of humour or sarcasm.

Leah and Mitch exchanged a look which clearly conveyed how they felt about her reply, until an ungodly shriek pierced the air. Instantly breaking into a run towards the source of the noise, she rounded a low building with her weapon ready to see Ash and the other dog locked in a curious butt-to-butt embrace, both salivating and whining, and wearing an exhausted look of shame. Terror evaporated into embarrassment and the small crowd dissipated to leave the dogs to have their private time in peace.

Within the hour they were plodding their ponderous return journey back to Sanctuary, hearts heavy with a sense of uneasiness at how these people had escaped the post-apocalyptic bingo of terrible events thus far.

LAYERS UPON LAYERS

The two men spoke quietly, despite their elevated station, for fear of being overheard. They had enjoyed a great deal of privilege, even more so after moving to the new camp, but the conversation they were having was one that didn't pay to publicise.

Everyone there was encouraged to report on the activities of others; guards reported on other guards as well as reporting their observations on the attitudes and behaviour of those under their dubiously named protection.

The two brothers whispered to each other, both freezing still and holding their breath when a noise sounded outside the room they were in. When the small sounds of a person walking down the corridor faded away they breathed out in unison and continued in a hushed whisper.

"How are we going to get the others to follow us?" the quiet one asked.

"We just take control and they will have to follow us!" his younger brother responded too loudly, receiving an angry shush to quieten him. "Some of them might try to protect him, but if we kill a couple the others will fold like origami."

Benjamin thought about it. He thought about it so long that he could almost feel Will's frustration at his own inaction quivering beside him; like it gave off an imperceptible hum.

"Maybe," he finally said, deep in thought, "but we have to pick who we trust very carefully."

Standing and squeezing his brother's shoulder with a fierce look of mixed excitement and pride, Will left the room to carry on as normal.

Leaning back on his bed, Benjamin's mind ran riot with the possibilities of what could go wrong. He disagreed with Richards on many things, but he couldn't argue that the man wasn't efficient at running the place. He enjoyed rank and its associated privilege, but deep down he knew he was just a guard dog wearing a fancy collar.

Could he even expect to do any better? Would his younger brother's tendency towards being impetuous jeopardise both of their lives?

With all these thoughts bouncing like a screensaver in his mind, he lay back to a restless sleep racked with tortured dreams.

And so began the race to seize control of the camp, although neither faction knew of the other's existence yet.

ROBIN HOOD

Before Leah and Mitch returned, a face that Dan hadn't seen before arrived at the gates of Sanctuary. From his chilly perch atop the battlements where, unknown to him, Leah had stood that morning, Dan watched as the sentry on the gate waved a familiar greeting to the man he obviously knew.

For the first time in weeks Dan missed having his equipment at his fingertips as he reached for his rifle and the zoom optic attached to it. Cursing silently, he was forced to rely on the mark one human eyeball to gather more information. All he could see from that distance was that the newcomer was a big man, barrel-chested and carrying something he couldn't fully make out. His inquisitive nature was piqued, and he jogged down the ancient stone steps for a closer look.

The distance really did not do the man justice. Dan was reminded of Bronson, the slaver he had faced so long ago. Just as that man, this newcomer to his rabbit hole, was a giant amongst normal humans. He stood at well over six feet but with such overt power in his upper body and arms which were wider than most men's thighs. The look was completed with the wildest and most fearsome beard Dan had ever seen; he marvelled at it with is mouth open, worrying that the man could conceal a weapon in the wiry mess hanging from his chin.

Seeing his stare, the man regarded him with a look of almost cold malevolence before the huge beard cracked open to reveal surprisingly white teeth.

"You must be this man I have heard of," he boomed in obviously Russian accented English.

Dan was frozen to the spot at being addressed directly, especially in an accent he was not expecting, after most people around him did not speak his language. Like a fool, he just stood still with his mouth still slightly open.

The big, white smile disappeared, and the wild man turned back to the gate guard and spoke in rapid French. Dan caught nothing of the exchange, but he guessed that his inability to speak English was being discussed. Gathering himself, Dan tried to play it cool despite the fear that the man may eat him.

"Dan," he said loudly, offering a hand to the beast towering above him. In truth, the man was only four inches taller but his sheer strength and girth made him look far bigger.

The bright eyes above the beard shot back to him before the teeth appeared again.

"So you *can* make words after all?" he asked loudly, mocking him. He went on before Dan could answer.

"I heard of your comings here," he said, taking the offered hand with a surprisingly gentle touch, the Russian accent permeating every syllable of his speech as he released his grip and waved his expansive arms to demonstrate his point. "And I would have come sooner only I had great works to do." With that he gestured at a brutal weapon rested against the wall. Dan gaped at it: a compound bow of such simple origin in stark contrast with its complex series of strings and pulleys. Glancing back to the man he saw no less than three different sized knives sheathed at his waist, and a quiver sprouting synthetically feathered arrows jutting out over his right shoulder.

"What are you?" Dan said with unintentional rudeness, instantly regretting his words. Luckily the feral giant before him took no offence.

Smiling broadly, he announced himself grandly, "I am Pietrovich, but you may call me Pietro. I came here to hunt in the mountains as I have done for every year. It is my… *otpusk?*" he struggled for the right word, snapping the fingers of his right hand. "My vacations?"

"You're here on holiday hunting?" Dan asked, mouth agape once more.

"Yes!" Pietro answered, glad that this simple man understood his meaning. "I hunt the boar in the mountains and woods, but now I spend much time hunting *volk* who have been made bold now."

Dan thought for a moment.

"Wolves?" he asked, hoping his guess was wrong.

"Yes. The wolves," he agreed seriously, deflating Dan's sense of safety. "They breed like the rabbit now, and come from the hills to take animals. This we cannot allow."

For the first time Dan noticed that the huge man was made to look bigger by the big, dark fur cloak he wore over his shoulders. Seeing his gaze fixed on it, Pietro smiled broadly again and explained.

"This was my first," he said as he smoothed the pelt almost lovingly like it was a living pet. "He was the big *Noche Volk*. I killed him with a single arrow, then his pack attacked me. They are much like us; their bravest warriors take the front rank in attack behind their leader, and the young, old and timid stay in the back. I killed three more before they ran from me."

He said it with passion, but no sense of inflated bravado came from behind the big beard. Dan absorbed what he had said. He had killed a huge alpha wolf, the night wolf as Dan guessed he had called him, then killed another three without mention of anything other than a bow and arrow. The train of thought was obviously not wasted on the big Russian, and he lifted the tail of the shabby black pelt to better show the brutal blades hung at his waist. The small smile of pride from under the wild facial hair told Dan the rest.

This beast of a man had killed four wolves with, well, not his bare hands, but damned well close enough. The awe and fear Dan felt in the presence of him mingled together and rendered him something close to star-struck. Unsure of what to say, he blurted out his next thought without applying the brain-mouth filter.

"We had a gamekeeper back home. He was called Pete too, but we didn't have any wolves," he said, instantly wincing at his 'I carried a watermelon' level of stupid things to say.

Pietro carried on the conversation for him, luckily. "I would like to meet this English Pietro!" he boomed, clapping an unnaturally large hand on Dan's shoulder and rocking him off balance. "Tell me, Englishman, have you ever hunted?"

Dan was unsure how to respond. He had hunted after a fashion, with shotgun and dogs to flush birds into the air, and later he had hunted men through battlefields and destroyed towns before swapping that battlefield for law enforcement. That was even before the world turned to shit and he had hunted men and dogs under a whole new set of rules. His hesitation gave Pietro room to continue.

"I shall take you, Dan. You will learn to shoot the arrows as I do."

Finding his tongue at last, Dan responded. "I'd rather find a decent supply of military weapons," he said almost sullenly.

"Ah!" Exclaimed the Russian, unperturbed at not having his offer graciously accepted. "I know a place you will come to see then."

WASTED EFFORT

Many miles to the north and slightly east of Sanctuary, a tired Land Rover was plodding steadily south. The four exhausted passengers, exhausted not so much through lack of sleep but pure travel weariness, were less alert than their usual natures dictated. They hadn't encountered another living person for weeks, and since the ambush they had avoided anything which looked like it offered even a hint of trouble. Their journey had been arduous, as they tried to keep away from the main toll roads where they could find themselves trapped and ambushed, instead keeping to the minor roads which were winding and often blocked.

Rounding a long, sweeping left-hand bend as they drove through countryside full of rolling hills and valleys, three of them were almost transfixed by the elegant beauty of a towering suspension bridge in the distance. The three included the driver, but not Paul who slept noisily in the back seat. Marvelling at the sheer height of it, Simon wondered aloud how many years and how many tonnes of metal it took to make such a bridge, and whether they thought it had been worth it when they had finished. Still, for now he had to admit that it was a thing of contrasting beauty to the green views surrounding it.

Leaning back and lapsing into a sad silence, he kept his thoughts private about how the bridge would eventually tumble to the earth far below it through a combined effort of nature's encroachment and a lack of human maintenance. Maybe one day someone, somehow, will look at the remains of the remarkable feat of engineering and imagine the civilisation that built it, much as their own ancestors did with the remains of roman bridges and buildings. A few miles further into the valley and the thoughtful silence had yet to be broken, but as they started to drive up a slight incline towards the start of the bridge, something made Lexi take her foot off the accelerator pedal and coast to a stop.

Opening the driver's door and stepping stiffly out, she raised her weapon to peer down the optic towards the cluster of buildings in the distance.

Sensing that the movement of the vehicle had stopped, Paul woke from his sleep to see Lexi aiming her weapon. Scrabbling to collect his own rifle he burst from the rear passenger door and threw himself down, asking in a shout what was going on.

His panic had caused a little amusement to the others, which put him in a bad mood mostly through embarrassment. Standing and dusting himself off, he asked again what was going on.

"Buildings ahead," Lexi said, her eye back to the optic. "Something looks out of place; there's a big green fuel tanker and what looks like some kind of armoured vehicle parked there. It looks completely out of place…"

Dropping her rifle abruptly, she turned to the others.

"Dan and the others were planning to get military vehicles from a base, weren't they? This could be them!"

From a rooftop ahead, two prone figures watched their approach. The man grunted and shoved his companion with his shoulder to indicate that he wanted the binoculars. She reluctantly handed them over in silence, even that small movement betraying the feline smoothness of her body.

Leo, le chasseur, watched in silence for a few seconds before asking the woman something in French.

"Same group, Sabine?" he asked in his gruff voice.

"Who knows?" she answered. "I didn't see that vehicle when they were together, but they may have been somewhere else. Either way, they don't look like they belong here."

With another grunt she couldn't decipher, Leo muttered, "Only a few days after the others were here? Too much coincidence." Then began to shuffle back from the ledge.

When they had both moved out of line of sight to the intruders, they straightened and Sabine found Leo staring intently at her.

"We take them anyway," he said. "I haven't had a good hunt in weeks."

All thoughts of self-preservation evaporated in the excitement that they may have, impossibly, caught up with their friends. Lexi repeated her thoughts that the military vehicle was exactly the kind of thing Dan would go for.

Driving straight up to the low buildings, she stopped the Land Rover and got out.

"Dan," she yelled, "Leah."

Simon shushed her, his face betraying his sudden fears growing in a knot in his stomach and replacing the infectious excitement he had felt moments before. Lexi's first instinct was to ignore him, but something inside her too felt wrong.

In unspoken unison, the four of them turned to get back in their vehicle and create space between the buildings and themselves; some instinctive feeling of distance meaning safety, like a height advantage.

Paul was behind her when she turned, so when he turned too he blocked her view. Looking worriedly over her shoulder she didn't see him stop, and collided heavily into his back. Before she could ask why, she saw his hands open and move slowly away from his weapons. Stepping to the side of him, she too froze.

Armed men were fanning out from behind their Land Rover, whilst two remained static using the big truck as cover over which to aim their weapons at them.

Not a word was spoken as their weapons were stripped from them, their every movement subject to scrutiny by men with fingers on triggers.

Still, the bearded, rough men said nothing to them but exchanged looks with one another to communicate. Paul watched as Lexi's arms were pulled behind her back and a zip-tie was pulled tight over her wrists. Her body arched with pain as the plastic bit into her skin, prompting Paul to step forward to intervene through instinctive protectiveness.

A rifle butt hit him in the head from behind. A short, sharp, professional jab designed more as a reminder than with the intention of doing any real damage. When he looked back to Lexi he saw the man who had cuffed her kick the backs of her knees and force her to the ground. He yanked her hair back and drew a dull, black pistol from his waist. Placing the barrel against her head, he looked Paul directly in the eyes and smiled. Shaking his head slowly, his point made, he looked down at his captive and smiled again.

RELUCTANCE TO CHANGE

By the time Leah, Mitch and Ash traipsed back in from their supply run the sun was beginning to sink below the hilltops. Dan met them at the gate having seen their approach; he was beginning to feel like a spare part as Marie was becoming annoyed at his fussing and frustration. He knew he was acting out because he was restless, now that the bubble of safety was becoming more transparent. His other option for company was to dictate his thoughts and knowledge to the annoying little wizard in his tower who believed that some notes on farming and survival would mean a damn thing when a raider came for his head with a machete.

The solitary sentry guarding the gate broke away from the constantly sullen look he gave Dan and spoke in French with the man leading the cart. Ash loped in as the heavy, foot-thick wood creaked apart, with his tongue lolling from one side of his mouth. He stopped panting as he looked up at Dan before flopping to the floor. Glancing up at Leah and forgetting to even welcome her back or ask a dozen other questions he had ready, he said, "What the fuck have you done to my dog?"

Leah blushed, much to his surprise, and Mitch's laughter made him turn to the soldier.

"The bugger got his end away the second we turned our backs," he said through laughter, which didn't seem like it had subsided much.

Looking down at his dog, who he suspected may already be asleep or close to it, he pushed that unexpected piece of information aside for now.

"Dirty bastard," he muttered before stepping around him.

He stepped closer to his two human friends and began to discuss what they had seen as the heavy creaking noise indicated the return of the doors to the securely locked position. The guard came to stand behind the returning escort and stared at them. Dan acted as though he hadn't noticed the man's presence and continued to speak, which irked him even more and made him shuffle his feet impatiently.

He didn't realise how much, until that moment, the man who lived on this gate annoyed him. He was short, not massively below average height but small enough for Dan to call him short, and his face seemed to constantly show a life of disappointing people. He disappointed Dan then by loudly clearing his throat.

As one, the three of them stopped speaking and turned to regard him coldly; this trio was not used to being interrupted.

To his small credit, the guard didn't waver under their combined gaze. That, Dan thought, was either foolish ignorance or bravery. He suspected the former.

"Guns," he demanded petulantly. Leah sighed and began to unsling her M4 until Dan held up a hand to stop her.

"You think you can hold back an attack with that piece of crap?" Dan asked quietly, pointing at his poorly maintained rifle slung on his shoulder. "No spare ammunition, just you with one gun? Is it even loaded?" he asked, the volume of his voice raising as he spoke. Stepping through the small gap between Leah and Mitch he took a step towards the smaller man to demonstrate his height advantage.

He knew it was petty of him to act the alpha male, and he recognised it was through frustration and inactivity, but he was on a roll now and if he was honest with himself, the guard had been pissing him off for some time. He would have noticed this sooner if he hadn't buried his head in the sand for a time after finding safety.

"They'll be keeping their weapons," he said with finality, and walked away. Leah and Mitch followed.

The guard took a step to follow them and opened his mouth to protest, but his path was blocked by a huge dog who had silently woken up and rose to face him. Ash merely cocked his head and regarded the man with curious intensity – like he was wondering what he tasted like – which was enough to dissuade him from pressing the matter any further.

The self-appointed guard was named Olivier, and proudly boasted that he had been a soldier in the 35th Régiment d'Infanterie. He had served with the French army that much was true, however, he chose not to mention that he was a junior non-commissioned officer in charge of a small catering unit and had spent his short career in the French armed forces on safe bases in his own country. He judged that this fact was irrelevant to his current standing as *Maréchal de Sanctuaire*, a title only he knew of.

These newcomers frightened him. They were not French to begin with, but the fact that their equipment and skills made his own seem paltry simultaneously offended and terrified him. They were treated well by Polly and the others, and only Olivier spoke ill of their arrival.

He spoke enough English to know for certain that Dan had just refused his rightful orders to relinquish weapons to his control, and had marched off blatantly flouting his authority.

Full of indignation and damaged pride he bustled off to find Polly and inform her of the actions of these dangerous interlopers.

~

Dan was filled in about the outlying farm, and specifically how vulnerable it was, and a more in-depth description was given about Ash's passionate tryst with one of the locals.

Still armed and armoured, they sat together and ate as they talked. They drew only a handful of curious glances, but most people saw nothing wrong with their appearance.

Others of their group drifted in after the bell had sounded in the tower, indicating that the evening meal was ready. Neil sat next to Dan heavily, intentionally bumping into him as he beamed a smile at the group.

"Alright, dickheads?!" he asked loudly. His sleeves were rolled up despite the low temperature and biting wind, and oil stains on his hands and arms were evident. Neil had been in heaven since they had arrived at Sanctuary, happily handing in his weapons and looking for food and a comfortable bed. He had established himself in a small apartment above a bar on the other side of the quay to the main central fort, and revelled in telling stories to his multinational audience in the evenings. His days were spent fixing things; from boat engines to his most recent project of helping a local man to fix the ailing waterwheel which rested in the fast-flowing stream coming down from the mountains.

"Neil," Dan said formally before turning back to the others. His attempt at keeping a straight face lasted mere seconds before his friends tickled his ribs to make his face crack. Shrieking like a child, Dan relented and greeted him more warmly before catching them all up on the events of the day.

It felt good for them to be together again. Even better to see some new faces join their group which was clearly having more fun than the majority of the population. A large contingent of the fishermen, and women, came in and the man at the front of their group nodded a fond greeting before sitting close by.

Dan's happy smile faded a little in worry. He suddenly saw himself from the outside perspective, and he looked like he was trying to take over. Just as this dawned on him, he saw Polly threading her way through the tables to catch his eye. He met hers, and she jerked her head to indicate that she wanted to talk in private. He rose, giving his excuses and asking Mitch to fill the others in on Ash's first girlfriend as he left the room.

He wasn't sure what he expected, other than to be berated for undermining the authority placed in the man given guard duty.

He wasn't expecting her to be smiling.

"Olivier came to me today with the most grievous of accusations," she said through her smirk. Dan said nothing. "He tells me that you threatened him, and took weapons into the town without his authority."

Dan snapped.

"His authority?" Dan scoffed. "Four children using bad language could get past him!"

Polly held up a hand to stop him. "Olivier is very proud of his military achievements, and not too long ago he was sat as you were in there with others crowding around him to hear stories of the wars he had been in. He did many brave things during the Balkans war, you know?"

Dan opened his mouth to respond, but his brain moved quicker than his tongue for once. Olivier, as he now realised the man called, must be either very young looking for his age or was a good five years younger than him. Dan served with the United Nations at the very end of the Balkans conflict when he was young, and he saw contact only once there.

"How old is Olivier?" he asked.

"I don't know," Polly answered, "maybe thirty?"

Dan thought for a second to be sure; certain in the knowledge that mathematics had never been a subject he excelled in.

"So he would have been born in the mid-to-late-eighties," he said, "and the fighting was over in Bosnia, other than a peacekeeping force which saw very little action, by about 2001. So Olivier claims he was at war when he was, what, fifteen or sixteen? Not even the *French* would send kids on a UN deployment!"

Polly's face dropped as she contemplated the basic facts. It didn't occur to most people to check these facts, but Dan could smell bullshit from a distance.

"What's the French for *Walter Mitty*?" he asked, earning a confused look from her.

"He's lying. He can't have been in contact in the Balkans because he would have been too young to be sent there, if he was even *in* the armed forces that is," Dan finished.

"That's not the reason I wanted to talk to you," Polly said, hurriedly changing the subject. "Although I want to explore that a little more another time. I have spoken with Pietro and I'd like you and Leah to meet with me."

Now Dan knew the reason for her seeking him out, and a flutter of excitement burst inside him. Pietro had told him of a military base in the mountains which sparked his shopping instincts. On any other day he wouldn't have known how to raise the subject, but after Polly's questions about protecting Sanctuary coupled with the town's only 'soldier' making a fool of himself, he saw their opportunity to ensure their safe haven remained that way.

He tried to imagine how that would play out. Most people would not raise any objections as far as he could guess, as they mostly went about their daily business with a smile of satisfaction. He would need to recruit more people to keep watch, would need to train them with guns, would need to organize a proper defence and guard rotas on top of training the whole town on what to do if the alarm was raised, but he was confident. Only a few flies would look to get in his ointment, but they could be easily persuaded otherwise.

He hoped. First, he had to do the mother of all resupply runs.

THE THREAT WITHIN

Richards was not a patient man, in spite of the fact that he believed he radiated an aura of calm competence. Every day his desk was growing more and more littered with reports of overheard conversations, suspected gatherings and rumours. Most were pathetic and pointless, submitted by low-level guards looking for a rise in status by getting their names noticed, but he couldn't decipher the rest; or at least he couldn't be bothered to. He muttered to himself about sorting the wheat from the chaff, earning an unsolicited response from his assistant who was sat nervously opposite him having brought the compiled reports.

"What? Oh, nothing," Richards replied absent-mindedly. "What do you make of this rubbish, Max?" he asked, tossing the papers in his hand onto the desk.

Max was as anxious as ever in the presence of the man in charge, who he felt, with utter certainty, was insane. It was not only his dictator-like attitude towards the cogs in his machine – the little people – but his personal fixation with him. He had to be at his desk seven days a week, and could only go back to his private quarters in the guard barracks when Richards dismissed him, often late into the evenings.

His elevated status offered perks; he had good food, he had no manual labour, and he was able to shower with hot water every day. Richards insisted on that fact, which caused him concern, and he was well-dressed in freshly pressed, fashionable shirts every morning.

He wouldn't see these perks as a cause for concern, if it weren't for the fact that his duties weren't exactly strenuous and he had no former qualifications or experience which singled him out as worthy to be the personal assistant of the commander. He was picked out of the crowd one day and elevated to his position of authority and privilege seemingly on his appearance alone.

Max knew he was a good looking young man. He was just coming up to twenty-three years old, and having been a keen sportsman from when he could walk, he was fit and slim. His dusty blonde hair was always roguishly perfect, even when he first woke, and his casually impressive appearance had always made other people jealous. Just another winner of the genetic lottery, he guessed, even though his mother used to embarrass him by saying how beautiful he was.

Now he was worried. Of late he had seen Richards's calm exterior cracking, and the stress pouring out from underneath like a volcano. Max had himself written the retrospective order for Richards to sign for the summary execution of a guard accused of assaulting a woman, and the cold fury he had experienced when it was dictated to him sunk deep into his bones.

No doubt about it, he was the personal assistant to a madman. Clearing his throat, he tried to answer in a non-specific way so as not to suffer the wrath of the man in front of him, and hopefully not to give an opinion which could result in the deaths of 'the little people' as Richards called the general population of survivors.

"I think most of it is probably just unsubstantiated rumours," he started in small voice, earning a snap from Richards to speak up. "Rumours," he said again, more loudly this time. "Gossip overheard and guards adding two and two to make six, sir," he said, trying to placate the rising anger in the man opposite him. A tense moment of silence hung heavily in the air between them until Richards snapped forward and stood.

"I'm sure you're right," he said, "but still, I want you to sort through all this rubbish and bring me anything I need to know. This is your highest responsibility now." He paused to fix him with an intense gaze, eyes boring through the younger man. "I'm relying on you, Max. You are my rock amongst this sea of inadequacy," he finished with a wistful gesture towards the world outside his office.

Fighting down the urge to shudder, Max responded,

"Yes, sir. I will."

Max sat at his desk for hours, well into the evening, sorting the papers into separate piles relating to their subjects. He kept notes on the sources of information in order to track the reliability, seeing if anything was corroborated by another person which would upgrade their reliability score.

By the end of his first day as an impromptu intelligence analyst, he had created the beginnings of a web with links between suspicious people and reliable guard information. Suddenly realising that his work could be instrumental in not just the subjugation of the others living there, but could be used to justify more executions, he stopped working. Slowly tidying away all the papers and burying his web chart at the bottom of a drawer at his desk, he racked his brains about what to do next.

Mere minutes later, Richards emerged from his office and looked around, seeing Max still working away. Max slid a piece of paper under a loosely stacked sheaf to keep unreasonable eyes from detecting it.

"Got anything for me yet?" Richards asked hopefully

Leaning back with a feigned stretch of exhaustion, Max answered him tiredly, "No Sir. Mostly low-level gossip from guards looking for advancement is my guess. A lot of them are telling tales on each other for what they think is leniency on workers."

Richards seemed satisfied with that. Scornful, but satisfied all the same.

"Well resume tomorrow," he said. "Join me for a drink?" he said and walked back towards his office without waiting for a response. It was an order, delivered as a question out of well-bred manners. But an order all the same.

"Two minutes, sir?" Max replied. "I just want to finish reading these last couple of reports to put it to bed."

"Of course," Richards answered over his shoulder, "I shall pour."

Sighing at the prospect of having to drink scotch, a drink he didn't even like, with a man who frightened him and listen to old stories, he quietly retrieved the paper he had secreted.

Following the snaking lines of ink from various sources back to the subject, his eyes settled on the most prevalent name.

Steve.

CONSOLIDATION

Polly sat first, inviting Dan, Leah, Mitch, Marie and the still oil-stained Neil to join her. She showed none of her usual prevarication and launched straight in to what was bothering her.

"Since you arrived, I have had concerns about the world outside of this valley," she began surprising nobody. Dan remembered clearly the look of horror on her face when he had recapped the last nearly two years of their collective existence. "Up until you showed up, our biggest worries had been weather and wolves; and neither have been particularly troublesome—"

A knock at the door interrupted her and all five of them looked up expectantly as Victor walked in without waiting for a response to his knock. Perhaps he felt his presence was expected and the knock only served as an announcement. He was expected, as Polly fired a rapid sentence at him in French. He nodded and pulled up a chair to bridge the gap between Polly and her audience; no doubt an intentionally calculated move as Victor didn't seem to be an outwardly emotional man, or that he had studied other humans and tried to join in their game.

"I've just told Victor that I was catching you up on our thought process," she said to the people who spoke little to no French.

Interesting, thought Dan, shooting a meaningful glance at Marie to see it instantly reciprocated. Both believed there was a structure behind Polly's seemingly unchallenged leadership of the town, now they felt certain that her private think tank was pulling at least some strings.

"And we both agree that the outside world has devolved into anarchy, which seems to have overlooked us. So far," she said, leaving the last words hanging heavy.

"You mean the group we had to run from before we got here?" enquired Neil innocently

"Groups," Victor corrected. "And yes. The groups that took almost all of your supplies, nearly killed someone you describe as your best fighter, and made you run." His words were unintentionally harsh, more out of a lack of tact than any attempt to goad them. His almost detached sense of social skills reminded Dan of Emma when they had first rescued the timid scientist, except Victor wore a cloak of undisguised intellectual superiority which made him hard to like. If anyone would have reared up to spit back a retort to the implied criticism, Dan would probably have put money on it being himself. Or Leah. Mitch was, as always, implacably hard to annoy. To his small surprise, Marie was the first to speak, only she did so in a quietly precise voice which Dan recognised as a warning sign. With a small smile, he sat back to watch the exchange.

"Victor?" she said almost sweetly, wearing a disarming expression. "How well would you, or anyone here for that matter, have fared against a group of people who are obviously well trained and under effective leadership?"

Victor realised the situation he had just walked headfirst into; a disagreement with a woman who was not accustomed to losing disagreements. Holding his hands up to better explain and soften the meaning of his last statement too late, she fired.

"The five of us in this room could seize control of this town, even the pregnant one," she added sarcastically. Leaning forward in her chair as far as her swelling midsection allowed, she continued her rant with a captive audience. Dan hadn't had chance to fill her in on the conversation with Polly, so she didn't know that Polly was coming – had probably already come – round to the idea of fortifying Sanctuary. He also knew that interrupting the future mother of his child was not a good idea.

"You've got one soldier," she carried on, "and from what we hear now he probably wasn't even a real soldier. So if you don't think the outside world is a dangerous place then maybe we should leave?"

Polly almost had to stand and wave her arms to halt the beginning of the tirade.

"I agree entirely," she said, stopping Marie midway through forming her next sentence.

"We are reliant on our walls, but walls need to be defended and our current strength – if it can be called that – seemed sufficient before your arrival." She paused, unsure how to make her next point delicately. She finally decided on bluntness.

"And the simple fact is that our biggest threat from other people is because of you coming here. If you were followed..." She paused again to swallow and consider the wording of her next sentence. "I worry that you may have brought that violence of the outside world to us."

Marie was the first to break the silence, embarrassed at her outburst and hostility. In truth, she was starting to lose control of her emotions at times and couldn't quite convince herself that it was all pregnancy related; she had to accept that the rollercoaster they had been on before landing in safety had caused her more stress than she wanted to admit to anyone. Least of all Dan, who she suspected had been close to the edge, if not leaning precariously over it when Leah had dragged him back to her.

"I agree, I'm sorry", she said. "We can't blame you for not being prepared for what's out there – you didn't know it was like that until we turned up."

Dan picked up her train of thought.

"I'm surprised that you haven't, though," he said. "We came across four hostile, armed groups within a matter of a few hundred miles of here and I don't think you can hide forever, especially as you are literally broadcasting your location for everyone to hear."

That caused a look to be exchanged between Polly and Victor. Clearing his throat, the professor answered the question.

"We put a stop to that over a month ago," he said, surprising the others that he and Polly had obviously considered their vulnerability and not taken any action other than to stop advertising their presence.

"And now," said Neil thoughtfully, "you want to take a more *proactive* approach to staying safe?" he enquired gently with emphasis.

Another look between their hosts.

"Yes," they both answered at once.

"Dan," Victor said, "your group have the skills and experience that we have been lacking and, until recently, we did not understand that we needed an answer to violence."

Dan agreed wholly. He was so deeply ingrained in his cynicism and fear of outsiders now that he saw no other way to be: violence had to be met with overwhelming violence. Hit them before they can hit you. His mind flashed back to a conversation with Penny so long ago that it was in a different world. He told her that sometimes violence was the only answer.

Concentrating again on the immediate, he told the room about the military base discovered by Pietro which didn't come as a surprise to anyone present.

Word travelled fast, even without social media and phones, it seemed.

For the next hour, they worked out the logistics of travelling there and hopefully bringing back all the toys Leah wanted to fulfil the plan which had kept her awake for weeks.

THE STORM

The weather closed in on them with such malevolence that it kept all but the most resilient of people safely ensconced inside. It rained for days on end, non-stop; the kind of heavy, relentless rain which soaked a man to the skin in minutes and with it came the cold, bitter winds blasting in from the sea.

The fishing parties were driven ashore and could not risk braving the roiling swells for weeks, even though the fishermen and women were unperturbed by rain. The risk of a boat capsizing was too great to take, especially as any rescue would not be coming. Even fishing by line from the sea wall became too perilous as waves crashed over the parapet day and night.

Dan was frustrated as he always was when he was stuck inside. His impatience stemmed from having a task which needed undertaking, and his inability to accept a timetable which didn't comply with his 'now' principle. His impatience and frustration poured out through pure sullenness, and Marie made her feelings clear on the matter. She had her own worries; not that she didn't feel like ensuring the protection of the town was a priority, but more that her daily dosage of aspirin became a constant reminder that both she and the baby she carried were drawing closer to the most fraught and dangerous time to both of their lives. The course of gentle blood thinners would escalate towards the end of her now very obvious pregnancy and culminate in doses of warfarin leading up to her estimated due date in about four months' time.

His impatience and her short temper made for the occasional explosive disagreement which could be heard in detail by anyone within an immediate proximity to their room.

Leaning back on her bed with Ash asleep on his back by her feet, legs in the air, Leah smiled to herself. Taking the outsider's view to their current argument, it was clear to her that both were of the same opinion, only that both wanted the notion accepted in their own words and neither would budge. They were arguing the same point to each other, and for whatever reason neither could see it. Intervention crossed her mind, but was dismissed as far too much effort would be required.

All she could do was bide her time. She used the ancient stone staircases twice daily to sprint up before walking back down and repeating the process; each time followed by an amused but uncomprehending Ash. This kind of explosive exercise rang a small bell in the back of her mind from before. From her old life. Something about high-intensity cardio or something, but the catchy name no longer mattered. She raised her heartrate until her lungs threatened to burst on each slow descent to ground level, only to be forced back up on the next sprint. Dan even joined her some days, desperate for some form of physical punishment to focus his mind. They had no breath to speak to one another as the precious breath was required to replenish the oxygen burned from their muscles, but the companionship felt comfortable in its familiarity. Every day she would sit with Mitch… when she could find him. He disappeared for hours on end and was rarely seen joining them for an evening meal. The two went over in minute detail what should be on their wish lists. There was only so much planning they could repeat without the weather softening and allowing them to break cover.

Much further north, beyond the mountains which cut off the small section of the continent from the rest, a dark Land Rover drove slowly down a muddied track. The mud was cloying and ankle-deep now, and as the vehicle pulled to a stop close to a low building, the driver jumped down to land her clean boots heavily in a thick puddle. Cursing to herself she squelched to the door with her head tucked low against the howling wind. Standing to her full height as she emerged into the dry cocoon of the poorly lit room, she shrugged off her heavy black coat and shook the rain from it.

The three men around the table, all looking down on a paper map weighted at the corners, looked up at her arrival before bending their heads low again. She stalked towards the muttering sounds coming from the group and asked for an update. Two of the men glanced at each other before the taller one spoke.

"What we heard from their radio transmission, before it stopped broadcasting, leads me to believe they are here," he said gruffly, pointing the tip of a much-sharpened knife onto the south coast. The woman did not know where their current position was in relativity, but in this group she was already at risk of scorn from all but the leader so she kept that small ignorance to herself. He had elevated her position to one of power over others and the ingrained military sexism annoyed her, although not as much as it annoyed the men who now had to answer to her.

"And your plan?" she asked him confidently.

He thought on that for a moment.

"Do you think we can assault this place, Sabine?"

She knew the question was asked intentionally to showcase her authority, and she played along.

"We think this place is fortified, do we not?" she responded, meeting his gaze. He nodded.

"Then instead of trying to break in by force, maybe we try another way?" she said suggestively.

Leo, le chasseur, regarded his two subordinates briefly before quietly asking for the room. They shot glances at each other, at the woman, then walked out into the appalling weather without another word. Leo liked Sabine, the cat-like woman who matched his ruthlessness. She had brought supplies, fuel, weapons and nearly thirty men and women to his group and offered a deal. She filled in many of the blanks in his knowledge about this group of English who so imperiously wandered into his territory but resolutely refused to die. Pouring two glasses of something from a bottle he offered her one and gestured for her to sit with him.

"You mean to suggest subterfuge over force?" he enquired, suspecting that she held a tactical view. Unlike any of his men, she knew how to be sneaky.

"Yes. You want to chop down the tree, whereas I would suggest letting it rot from the inside."

A cruel smile appeared on his face as he raised his glass to her in small salute of her suggestion.

"And the prisoners?" he asked. "Do they feature in this *rot*?"

Smiling and leaning back in comfort she took a sip of her drink. "I'm sure they can be useful," she said with a cruel smile matched only by the man opposite her. "They can be used to unsettle them first, then..." She paused. "...a cheval de Troie," she finished.

Leo smiled wider. "A Trojan horse?" he repeated, "This, I like."

ALL ALONG THE WATCHTOWER

If leaving the safety of their walled town for an extended supply run was an impossibility until the period of bad weather broke, then the least Dan could do was focus on issues closer to home.

Much to the evident disgust of Olivier who stood in his usual spot by the heavy wooden gates, Dan strode past him without even acknowledging his presence and opened the room – little more than a broom cupboard – which served as an armoury using the key Polly had given him. Both he and Leah were kitted up as warriors once more, and in addition wore heavy waterproofs over the top of their equipment which had grown tighter given their evident comfort inside a safe zone. Dan hadn't replaced his lost and destroyed carbine since it had inadvertently saved his life by blocking the axe blow which would have likely severed his head, so now he retrieved their only surviving battle rifle chambered in the heavier 7.62 calibre. Where they were going, he needed to check out the vantage point with that kind of weapon anyway.

He couldn't shake the feeling of being watched ever since Pietro told him about the wolves that stalked the mountains surrounding them, and that fear was further compounded when Leah returned to corroborate the story from the inland farm. The fact that he was flanked by his own dangerous animal didn't register any irony in him, but his trademark shotgun strapped to the back of his equipment vest served as reassurance against the mysterious and primeval threat.

Braving the stinging rain blowing in unpredictable gusts from the sea, they left the enclave without ceremony and put their heads down to begin the climb.

In perfect weather, it would take someone of their fitness maybe thirty minutes to reach the high summit overlooking Sanctuary, even carrying weapons and equipment. With their heads tucked low and their footing unsure on the wet, rocky path, it took them closer to an hour. By the time the last false crest on the ground ahead fell away to reveal the base of the ancient stone tower, they were both exhausted and soaked to the skin despite their heavy coats. Ash, in contrast, was also soaked but seemed happy enough for the exercise. Shaking himself noisily at the door of the circular structure, he waited patiently for someone to let him in, no doubt intending to perform a more thorough shake when safely in a dry room.

Polly had briefed Dan about their barely-resident and cagey hermit, Claude, and offered to accompany them. Hearing that Claude spoke passable English, Dan politely declined the suggestion of a chaperone and saw Polly's evident relief at not having to brave the elements.

In no doubt at all that Claude would have seen them coming and had at least thirty minutes warning of their arrival, Dan raised his eyes to the windows that began on what he guessed was at least the third floor and shouted out a loud greeting.

Silence answered his call.

Not true silence, because the howling wind raged around them and the sound of rain hitting their waterproof clothing and equipment sounded like sporadic hail stones, but at least silence reigned form inside. Just as he was about to shout again, the unmistakable sound of a heavy bolt sliding back permeated the maelstrom outside and the door creaked open slightly. Nobody appeared in the doorway, and only darkness showed inside. Ignoring any sense of foreboding they might have felt under different circumstances, all three bundled inside.

What they found was not what they were expecting. It was as though they had stumbled, wet and dripping and heavily armed, into the cosy set of a bedtime story reading. A pair of comfortable rocking chairs sat in front of an open fire, one looking indented and well-worn where the other seemed untouched but for the layer of dust coating it, and little else adorned the circular room. A high wooden bench served as what appeared to be a kitchen, pallets of tinned food were stacked in neat rows against the wall behind it, and a wooden staircase wound upwards into the ceiling high above.

As Dan took a slow circle to drink in the unexpected ambience, the door slammed noisily and the bolt slid home again. Fighting down the instinct to treat this as a threat, Dan made himself turn slowly and regard their new neighbour.

Seeing a short, grizzled veteran of a man with a chest-length grey beard and suspicious eyes, Dan again forced his face to show his intent and not his reaction. *First contact protocols*, he thought with a hidden smile.

"Bonjour Claude," he began in appalling French, "Je m'appelle Da—"

"I know who you are," Claude interrupted in good English, before the unreadable look on his face softened slightly. He turned to Leah, and the beard revealed something of a sad smile.

"And I have seen you too, *mon chéri*." Leah smiled sweetly in return, and held out a hand to the old man whilst somehow managing to convey a look of embarrassed apology for how she looked.

Claude took the offered hand gently, and bent to kiss it with such an old-fashioned display of manners that Dan felt instantly boorish. There was zero, utterly no, feeling of inappropriateness in Claude's behaviour towards Leah, and both were struck by the obvious sense of paternal admiration he radiated.

"My name is Claude," he said, "you have heard stories of the crazy old man on the hill? Yes? Well I am him," he said with a smile of humour now, making an introductory jest at his own expense. Greetings over, Claude clapped his hands suddenly making everyone jump.

"Now! Get off these wet clothes and hang them by the fire to dry," he ordered them. Obeying, both stripped off their outer layers and equipment to place them on the wooden pegs by the hearth as Claude disappeared upstairs only to return momentarily with heavy blankets to wrap around their shoulders.

Instantly at ease and welcomed, they hovered by the fire as a metal teapot was hung in the flames to boil.

Dan eyed up the chairs, his senses pricking at something not being quite right, unable to yet articulate the thought knocking on his brain.

"So," Claude said again, joining them to warm his hands at the fire, "you want to take the defence of this town seriously?"

This unexpected clairvoyance saved Dan a lot of uncomfortable small talk – he liked a person who got straight to the point. Opening his mouth to speak, Dan closed it again as Leah answered first.

"Yes. How did you know?" she said sweetly, playing along with the tone of his greeting to her.

"Because, *mon chéri*, I watch you most mornings looking over the walls. I see you planning where to put the guns, and where to attack from. I saw this too when we first came here and nobody listened to the crazy old man," he said with another depreciating smile.

"We?" Leah probed gently, pressing her advantage.

"My wife and my granddaughter," he replied, eyes sad and glistening. "Both succumbed to illness, sadly," he crossed himself, the genuflection autonomous and subtle.

Placing a hand on his arm Leah offered her condolences.

"My wife was already very sick, but my sweet Claudette – my namesake as you would say – she caught a fever and did not recover. Both are buried outside, and I never left this tower since the day she joined her *grand mère*. I keep watch over them and the town below."

A moment of silence prevailed, during which everyone present tried to convey their sadness and respect. Until Ash shook himself again and settled at their feet to monopolise the heat from the fire, breaking the tension of the moment with a comedy deftness no human could pull off.

Laughing gently, the three people relaxed and Claude invited them to sit. Hesitating, unsure how to word his request, Dan suddenly realised what had piqued his senses about the seating situation.

"That's your wife's chair, isn't it?" he asked carefully.

Relieved that someone understood him, Claude smiled again. "Yes. Nobody has ever sat in it, but I would be honoured if you would, *chéri*," he said, turning to Leah who graciously accepted the offer with a sad smile.

Dan sat on the rug next to his dog whilst the girl carefully perched on the unused rocking chair and settled back. The kettle began to whistle, and over coffee the three of them discussed the plans to keep watch over their safe haven.

EYES ON

From a similar vantage point high on the cliffs opposite the tower and overlooking the wet, windswept town, one of Leo's most trusted men shivered in the storm.

He had performed this same task in Afghanistan, in Africa on the Ivory Coast, and a dozen other territories he hadn't known much about, nor could he accurately point to on a map.

His job was simple; he was a watcher, and sometimes he was a killer at great distances. There was something about his stone-cold psyche that made him perfect for this role, and the training and years of experience had only served to harden those traits in him to a granite-like veneer. He barely blinked, barely spoke, needed little in the way of comfort and never complained. He never asked too many questions either, and that endeared him to his superiors greatly. Throughout his long years in the vaunted French Foreign Legion, his demeanour perfectly fit the mysterious air that followed those soldiers everywhere they went, prompting young recruits to stop and stare in awe as they strode past.

Allowing the focus of his left eye to fade away he concentrated through his right down the long scope of his PGM Ultima sniper rifle. He had carried this rifle for a long time, and it had been with him on four continents now, not that he could recall each individual country – only the targets. There were newer weapons issued to the Légion Étrangère, but being something of a celebrity among the elite troops, his stubborn refusal to part with the weapon had been tolerated. It wasn't that it was better, just that it was *his*. The bulky metal and plastic gun was part of him, and he could wield it with near perfection.

It wasn't just his accuracy with the rifle that made him so effective, but his attitude towards his task: he was told to watch, so he watched. Failure wasn't an acceptable outcome to him, and only once had he failed. He allowed that one missed shot to sting his soul forever, as the tribal leader he intended to hit bent down suddenly allowing time for the bullet travelling the distance between barrel and target to slice through his shoulder and into a child behind the warlord. That moment would never leave him, not for sadness at the killing of an innocent, but for the fact that he failed where he had never failed before.

Scanning the ramparts of the medieval town walls far below his uncomfortable hiding place high on the cliff, his crosshairs showed glimpses of activity in between the squalls of rain which temporarily blinded his tiny window into the lives of the town's inhabitants. Few people showed themselves since the weather turned vile, not that he hadn't been prepared for a long and uncomfortable wait, despite still shivering through four layers of clothing and equipment. Continuing his methodical scan of the view below, the small and slow movement of the rifle barrel pointed his zoomed view to the lonely, round tower on the cliff opposite him. He could barely see in this weather at that distance, much less have any hope of making a successful shot, but another break in the stinging rain gave him a snapshot of two people outside the structure. One taller than the other, both unmistakably carrying weapons. This was a development, as the French sniper had yet to see anyone who offered him any threat. Le chasseur had briefed him about one person specifically - the man with the scarred face who had escaped their unit when their only sniper was deployed to protect a scavenging run.

Waiting patiently, barely moving other than to slowly inch the barrel to follow the pair's progress down the slippery path back to the town and to wiggle his toes and tense the muscles of his calves periodically to stimulate blood flow to his feet, he tracked their progress until they were close enough to make out more detail.

The man was carrying a rifle capable of reaching his position, not that the shot could be made easily in this weather, and he would surely have time to kill him three times over as he was already sighted in. The man also had a big dog following him, which seemed happy enough despite obviously being soaked to the skin. More curiously, he saw that the other person with the man was actually a young girl, even though she was dressed up like a soldier and carrying an automatic weapon. His trained eye noted that the way she carried herself indicated an ability to use the weapon.

He also made one small detail out as the man turned his head up to speak aloud when he reached the gates. He saw a faint, pink line running down the left side of the man's face over the eye, accentuated as the exposed skin of his face was pale and drawn in the appalling conditions.

Satisfied that he had accomplished enough of the mission parameters to justify withdrawal given the worsening weather, he continued his emotionless routine scanning of the town until nightfall, when he silently withdrew from the ridge and began the long journey to extraction.

FIRE SALE: EUROPEAN STYLE

The plan was ready, having been assessed and reassessed so many times due to the weather keeping them prisoner. When the endless series of storms finally broke, the heightened sense of excited anticipation buzzed throughout the town, as it was widely known what the newcomers had been asked to do.

This was an intentional display of public support by Polly, and an ingenious one in Dan's opinion: she was telling the town that the newcomers had brought abilities they needed, and were now willing to perform a task outside the walls for the benefit of everyone. Public support was not a problem, bar one or two sullen looks and grumbled French complaints.

The team had been carefully picked in a theme of both Anglo-French diplomatic relations, and ensuring adequate protection remained behind to secure the town. Dan selected his obvious candidates with care, needing Mitch's military weaponry experience and Neil's mechanical engineering mind to break into things. Who to leave behind was the biggest worry, and in the end he chose Leah. She complained to him recently about being seen as a child again, and he thought this was the best opportunity to show the residents of Sanctuary that he trusted her to stand in his place. He left Adam with her, confident that he would follow her instructions and provide the support of a familiar face.

More importantly than who to leave behind was the question of who to bring from the existing population. Obviously, they were in need of strong hands to carry the goods they hoped to find, but the political move of adding French fighters to their protection detail was needed to show that trust was a door which swung both ways.

Despite protests from others, he insisted that Olivier join them. The idea was Marie's, which she made sure was presented as Dan's, and was a clever move to show inclusion of the man they all suspected was, to put it bluntly, completely full of shit. The insistence of his inclusion was designed twofold: to suss him out, and to keep enemies closer.

There had been a lot of whispering amongst the people safe within the walls, and each night when they convened for their evening meal, more and more of the multinational band of genetic mutation lottery winners joined them, indicating a full swing in their favour on the trust-o-meter.

Amongst the shy newcomers that evening was a dark-haired beauty who Dan had seen working in one of the tall, narrow buildings in the town. She was short – no taller than Leah in fact – but beneath the lowered head and curtain of wavy hair hid a strikingly beautiful, hawk-like face. Slightly hook-nosed, but with distractingly big, dark eyes she smiled and seemed almost embarrassed as she perched next to Mitch.

Dan figured it out immediately, as had Marie probably a few minutes or even days before he did, but Leah paused with a fork halfway to her mouth as the scene before her bounced around her brain like a series of errant synapses that couldn't quite get the flow right. Then it hit her. She was holding Mitch's hand.

She fought to swallow her mouthful whilst simultaneously blurting out her accusations about where he had been disappearing off to all the time, when the sudden duplicity of her actions made her inhale her food and cough noisily, silencing the room.

With streaming eyes and a look of shame as everyone had stopped to watch the girl choke, she stood and looked at Mitch but instead of voicing her accusations she simply released a strained burp. As her watchers in the immediate area fell about laughing she sat down, her face reddening through a mixture of embarrassment and momentary oxygen deprivation.

"Everyone," Mitch announced to the table in general, "this is Alita." He smiled broadly as he looked at her, totally unaware that she wished the ground would open up and swallow her whole.

Alita was a good few years younger than Mitch, and had yet to turn thirty. Originally from Spain, which in reality was just over a day's walk away from where they were on the southern coast of France, she had travelled all over the world as a scuba diving instructor. She had lived in the Maldives, the Philippines, Fuerteventura and Lanzarote, as well as working in the Caribbean and Australia. Of all the wonderful and exotic locations she had lived and worked, there was always something tugging at her heartstrings when it came to the southern coast of the country neighbouring her birthplace.

All of this she would have explained to the group who were obviously eager to know more about her, but the overwhelming fact about Alita was that she hated being the centre of attention, and didn't much like talking to strangers. True, she spent her life teaching strangers how to dive and leading tourists through the reefs and rocks she grew to know like she did the way around the town streets, but that was work. Mitch wasn't work and, as such, she now felt like running from the room because everyone was looking at her and expecting some sort of response to Mitch's introduction.

Slowly, she raised her free hand as the other still gripped Mitch's like a vice and gave a tentative wave in combination with a small smile.

That seemed to satisfy the inquisition, and the collection of smiles aimed at her relaxed a little. As talk of the plan unfolded, she was happy to melt back into comfortable obscurity and listen as Dan laid out the bones of the plan for the following day.

Before sunrise the chosen team assembled by the gates, shivering with the combination of inactivity and cold. The defenders were also standing by to watch the small exodus, and for some a familiar feeling of purpose returned to invigorate them despite the chill in the air. With very little ceremony, the heavy gates creaked open and the team filed out with Dan in the lead under the considerable shadow Pietro cast from the weak light shining over the ancient archway.

His question of why there were no modern vehicles in the town had been answered simply weeks before; they kept some vehicles a way inland under cover to try and preserve them for as long as possible. Under Polly and Victor's joint leadership, the absence of fuel-driven vehicles was also a tactical move to adjust the psychology of the population; without daily reminders of missing the trappings of their now extinct modern lives, they would let them fall from their consciousness more easily.

Forty minutes' walk for their small group found them at an industrial hanger-type building, where they loaded up into three small commercial vehicles and let them run at idle to warm the settled oil in their engines.

Dan detailed people for each vehicle, unwittingly intimidating some of the locals who, until that point, did not realise they were undertaking a military operation.

Simple rules were set, actions on different situations arising were reiterated, and the order to move was given. Pietro drove the first vehicle, complaining good-naturedly about having to drive as he felt it made them soft.

"Would you prefer to carry a couple of large machine guns on your back?" Dan asked him.

"*Biz problema!*" Pietro retorted ebulliently, before remembering his audience and adding. "This would be simple".

"And the ammunition to feed them?" Dan pressed.

Pietro paused, evidently giving thought to the additional weight.

"Maybe this time it is good to drive," he said reluctantly.

Leading the carefully-moving convoy of three, with Mitch in the rearmost vehicle as the most trustworthy and capable, Dan checked in intermittently via the radios they had recharged for the first use since their ignominious flight to safety months before.

Dan's eyes flashed to high points, to anything on the roadside which caught his attention, to possible ambush sites. The increase of tension felt both familiar and exhausting.

The only source of discontent was Ash: he had to pick the only day for months when he was in a confined space with others to release a series of noxious smells, each time looking simultaneously innocent and offended at the reactions around him.

By the time the sun hit its peak they had arrived without incident or sign of life outside of their caravan.

Dan stepped down from the cab, took a lungful of unpolluted air, and stretched his back, feeling that old sensation of a compressed spine from too long in a car.

Looking behind as the others emerged, he caught the eye of Olivier. Making the quick decision whether to leave him with the others as protection or take him along; he decided to keep him close. Making the hand signals for 'on me' and 'rally point' he kept Olivier in his sight to see how he responded. If he were the infantryman he claimed to be, then his response to these silent instructions, in any language the world over, would be instantaneous.

They weren't. Mitch saw the signals and reacted, as did Neil, but Olivier looked around confused. Unsure, he walked tentatively towards Dan.

Catching Neil's eye, Dan indicated that he should stay put and guard the vehicles and received immediate confirmation that his orders were understood. He returned the long battle rifle to the cab of the lead vehicle as it would be useless in the confined spaces he expected, instead relying in his sidearm and the shotgun on his back.

Leading a team of four and a half; himself at the front with Ash pressed to his leg, Pietro behind followed by Olivier and Mitch at the tail, they began a slow circuit on foot of the base.

As in all military fashion for any continent, the base was a very unassuming and dull-looking fenced enclosure with a series of low buildings. The full lap took them almost another half hour, and solidified Pietro's assurance that the base was totally abandoned.

In essence, it was little more than a supply depot, but seeing as supplies were what they came for, Dan didn't see that as a problem.

Returning to the vehicles Dan called up Neil to dispatch the locks on the metal gates. Never one for subtlety, Neil pulled the ripcord starter on a disc cutter and illuminated their entrance with a flamboyant shower of sparks as the rusted metal gave way with a series of short, tortured shrieks. The gates creaked open on degraded hinges with a scream fit for a horror movie and Neil turned to Dan to give him a muted, but still characteristically 'Neil' bow of sarcastic welcome.

Indicating for Neil and his method of entry capabilities to fall in behind his small fire team of four – two soldiers, one hunter and one pretender – they began the laborious and time-consuming process of clearing each building one by one.

Starting at the low prefabricated hut intended as a gatehouse, they moved clockwise until each room on the base had been checked. Numerous times a boot had to be employed to open any door unwilling to accommodate them, and after Dan took three attempts to stave in one, Pietro decided to showcase his considerable size and strength and act as a battering ram.

After this display of bravado, Dan sized up one particular doorway then stepped back and nodded his head to the target for his Russian friend. Slinging his brutal bow diagonally over his torso, Pietro stood to his full height and flexed himself.

Rocking back, he lined up one huge boot intending to kick the entire door from its hinges and leave an impressive display of destruction to show this Englishman what he could achieve.

Dan, the victor of innumerable contests between man and locked door, smiled broadly in anticipation of exactly what he knew was about to happen.

The savagery of Pietro's kick did precisely what Dan predicted, and all professionalism disintegrated as the others erupted instantly into hysterics.

Furious with himself, with the door, with his audience, Pietro hopped on the spot as his right leg disappeared through the flimsy door which had swallowed the limb to mid-thigh.

Fighting away the tears, Dan stepped closer only to have to backpedal as the big Russian flailed about to free himself, effectively creating a hole in the door large enough to climb through. By the time he had extracted himself and attempted to regain some composure, Dan calmly leaned past him and tried the handle.

Pietro's red face burned out over his beard as the unlocked door swung out towards him, just as Dan knew it would. His anger at the failure and embarrassment dissolved immediately and he couldn't contain himself any longer, bursting out with uncontrollable laughter which they all tried to keep hushed.

Sometimes a genuine laugh was just more important than protocol.

This routine continued for a further hour, the intermittent sound of one of the team bursting into fits of giggles as the image of Pietro stuck in suspended animation halfway through the door popped back into their minds. If one of them released even the slightest of sniggers, another team member would be instantly infected by the hilarity and the ripple effect would debilitate them all again. The only one unaffected was Ash, who cocked his head and held his mouth closed to watch what overcame the people.

By now they were all so unconcerned with the sight of a decomposed body that the careful and reverent removal of a skeleton clothed in dusty rags was commonplace. With the exception of Olivier. From the horrified expression on his face at the various poses the former residents were stuck in, Dan became ever more certain that this man had seen none of the horrors of this world, let alone the ones from their previous lives.

Dan caught him stood over one dusty corpse and watched as he reached down to remove a filthy sidearm from a belt holster. Snapping his fingers for attention Dan watched as the Frenchman's head darted up as his hand whipped away like he was caught out. Dan shook his head, but realised that Olivier probably wouldn't understand. Stepping closer, he spoke in hushed tones.

"Clear first, scavenge later," he said simply.

A nod of embarrassed understanding was Olivier's only response.

Opening a protesting metal door in the largest building, a sickening stale odour burst from the dark entrance. This room must not have been as breezy as all the others, as it had retained a smell of decay. Flicking on a torch and raising his Walther in the other hand, Dan stood on the edge of the doorway taking cover automatically to prevent being silhouetted. Mitch stacked in behind him instantly, falling back on years of close quarter battle – CQB – training which he employed for real more times than he could remember. Neil stepped up close to Mitch's back and drew his Glock as Pietro watched on in confident amusement, yet still held his bow ready. In truth, Neil had learned far more in CQB and room clearance drills from Dan than he had in his military career. Olivier had no clue what to do. He lacked the knowledge or the confidence to stack up behind the others, and did not possess the good sense to get clear of the doorway.

Although overtly ignored, his indecision and obvious confusion was not lost on anyone present. Uttering a single word, the room clearance began.

"Seek," Dan growled with low urgency, and Ash rocketed low into the room to work.

A tense minute elapsed, during which they could hear the muted occasional sounds of the dog working the room with his nose for any trace of life or danger. Returning to the doorway with his snout covered in thick dust and cobwebs, he gave his report to Dan by way of a series of loud sneezes followed by a mouth open, tongue out look of satisfaction and anticipated praise.

"Ash says it's clear," Dan said, fussing the animal and reminding him what a good boy he was. Sneezing again Ash returned to his position by Dan's side and prepared to enter the room.

Of the six of them there, four including the dog had done this more times than they could ever count. One had skills which none of the others possessed, and the last was becoming ever increasingly exposed as a fraud.

Moving in with gun and torch raised, Dan muttered, "Go!" and slipped through the doorway, stepping fast to the right with Ash glued to his leg. Mitch flowed through simultaneously, peeling left. When they had gone through, Neil entered and stepped to the right of the door clear of the obvious funnel which would attract any fire.

The dog would have sounded off and returned at a rate of knots if anyone was inside, but this was real life and there were no respawns, so they stuck to the drills.

The moving pair – or trio really – flowed like water through the obstacles, around and between two large green military trucks, until they reached an internal wall at the far end of the dusty, and mostly empty, room. Calling the others up, they now assessed the next obstacle. This door was metal, reinforced at the lock, and far more substantial than anything they had encountered thus far, and as such held more promise. Trying the handle as a man never knew his luck, Dan found it secure. Holstering his weapon, he looked to Neil who silently turned and headed back to the doorway where he had left the disc cutter.

Dan held his disdain for Olivier in check and gestured for him to step up.

"Knock on the door and tell anyone inside that we're not going to hurt them. Tell them to open up," he said.

Olivier's confusion was evident, but he did as he was asked.

When no answer came, he looked questioningly at Dan again but the man simply nodded to him, then looked over his shoulder at Neil who fired up the tool and set to work cutting through the metal. Stepping back to give him space to work, the others waited as Neil sweated and grunted amidst a fountain of sparks. Ash took himself further away, fearful of the light and noise being more sensitive to the latter than all the others combined, and Pietro began to pick at his fingernails with a huge blade to pass the time.

Eventually, the sounds of tortured metal stopped and Neil stepped back. Mitch had found a length of metal, a heavy-duty tent peg by his best guess, and rammed the spike into the obliterated lock housing. Putting all his strength behind it, the doorway popped open and Dan sent Ash in again.

They had struck gold again. The floor was littered with the bodies of soldiers, all wearing the same uniform. Crouching and wiping the filth away from the insignia on the upper arm of the closest one, Dan gestured to Olivier to look.

"Military police," he announced, having deciphered the degraded writing.

Mitch took the metal spike to the nearest wooden crate, and after the lid was prised off he let out a long, low whistle which attracted the attention of the others.

Crowding around him, they looked down on a box crammed full of new and oiled assault rifles.

"Fucking bingo!" announced Neil, reaching down to lift one of the new HK416 rifles destined for who knew where.

"I read that the French were changing to these," Mitch said, jealous at having had spent years dealing with the unreliable and awkward bullpup design the British forces insisted he used.

"Clear the rest of the base then come back with the others," Dan instructed.

Within the hour, the remainder of the base was declared devoid of life, and all three of their vehicles were backed up to the doors of the building. A steady stream of two-person teams carrying the heavy boxes out into the sunlight was organized and the remainder of the room was being sorted and catalogued.

Although only a small armoury, they guessed that the addition of the crates of new assault rifles must have been in transit and likely escorted by the small detachment of military police who had succumbed whilst performing their final duty.

In addition to the new, and arguably best, assault rifles there was a rack of the older FAMAS which were destined for replacement. Dan also discovered the larger version of the HK, the 417, which fired the heavier 7.62 calibre and were configured as sniper rifles. A few under-barrel grenade launchers were found which could be fitted to the new rifles, but only one small metal tin of the 40mm bombs could be located, making them a very finite resource.

Neil was busy trying to coax one of the huge diesel-powered military transport vehicles back to life as the others worked, until Dan called for his help.

At the very back of the room, and secured behind a metal mesh barrier, sat two huge machine guns which harked from the days of the second world war, although their design had been much improved over the years.

"Bloody hell," breathed Neil when he saw the prize uncovered by the removal of ammo crates. Reverting to his favourite BBC English accent, he leaned close to the mesh to see them.

"Haven't seen a Browning," he pronounced it *brigh-ning,* "like that in years."

"A couple of fifty-cals would be nice," said Dan in wistful wonder, mentally calculating their destructive power in Leah's defence plan. "Cut the door for me?" he asked Neil.

"Cut it yourself," he responded, pointing to the disc cutter sat idle on the floor nearby. "Just don't cut your foot off or anything," he said before patting him on the shoulder roughly and returning to his resurrection project in the outer room.

"Thanks," Dan replied icily, earning a look from Ash as they were joined by Mitch, whose own appreciation for the destructive capability before him was evident. He told Dan he could clean them up and get them working, so long as they found enough ammo to make it worth their while lugging them back.

In truth, he was hoping for some smaller support weapons, but the big point-five-ohs would be a major addition to their prize fund.

Their vehicles were loaded with weapons and ammunition, a good third of their haul being given over to the big beasts and the massive ammo they fired.

As the last of the crates and lockers were prised open, Dan jumped at a sudden sound as Neil first fired the struggling engine of the truck, heard it whine tiredly before it barked into life and ejected a gigantic cloud of black, unburnt diesel into the room and caused a mass exodus of choking scavengers.

"Sorry chaps and chapesses!" he boomed from the doorway of the raised cab he stood proudly in, unable to hide his obvious pride and excitement. The main doors were hauled open to both clear the air and allow the big transporter to escape the dusty mausoleum.

Just as Dan was about to call for the saddle-up and return journey, Mitch excitedly jogged up to him.

"You've got to see this!" he blurted out, then turned on his heel and headed for the furthest corner of the room. Hauling a big canvas all the way back from a large crate, he shone his torch into the gap he had splintered into the wood.

Dan peered down and saw a dull green tube with a raised polygon at the end. As it dawned on him what he was looking at, Mitch couldn't contain himself any longer. "AT4s," he said, beaming an excited but borderline evil grin. "Anti-tank rockets."

Echoing Neil's earlier comment, Dan leaned back with his own smile.

"Bloody hell."

THE INSIDE MAN

Olivier took himself away after becoming bored with the menial task of carrying boxes. The people who, only a few months before, had viewed him with respect and often fear now ignored him or worse; they treated him as an equal.

Sullenly he wandered away, kicking at the overgrown thorns which had endured the lashing storms and cold temperatures. He regarded his new acquisition; the dirty sidearm caked with dirt which he lacked the sense to realise was the remains of its previous owner. He guessed the gun wouldn't fire in its current state, but he enjoyed the feeling of holding it. He wandered clear around the back of the big building where everyone else still contributed to the collective cause.

Had he been the soldier he had told everyone he was, he wouldn't have been looking at his feet and sulking. He would have noticed the trodden grass and – had he been half the man that Dan and Mitch were – he would have sensed that he wasn't alone.

By the time he realised he had made a mistake, the undergrowth to his left rose up and clamped a powerful arm around his neck, stifling any sound he could have made instantly. As terror hit him hard in the chest, the undergrowth to his right also came to life and easily pulled the rifle and sidearm from his hands without any obvious resistance before it sank with his slow and controlled descent to the ground, and placed its own camouflaged face in front of him.

The eye contact made him freeze, although the arm around his neck had already done most of the job. There was something in those eyes, some primal fear made him stay very still in some genetically predisposed, hard-wired self-preservation way; as a rabbit would do when a bird of prey cast a shadow over the grass ahead.

He stared into those eyes, and knew he was about to die.

"Quiet now," growled the monster before him in French, "do as I say and you will live."

The three trucks they had brought as well as the newly reanimated military transport were loaded and secured. Dan called everyone in and addressed the group in simple, short sentences, pausing occasionally for Pietro to translate his words. From the smirks on the faces of the others, he was certain the big Russian was adding some artistic license to his speech, but he let it ride.

He told them they had done well, that they should rest a short while and eat something before they headed back.

"Tonight, you'll be home in your own beds, and Sanctuary will be safe." He smiled broadly, not because he was a happy man as such, but more that he knew his facial expressions would need no translation. He climbed onto the bonnet of the big military truck and scanned a 360 out of habit. Whenever he gave other people a rest break he automatically stood watch over them, sacrificing his own downtime for the comfort of everyone else. That's just what leaders did. Ash sat on the ground and watched him, as Mitch put one foot on a large wheel and hauled himself up to the vantage point.

"Impressive swag," he mused aloud, gaining a grunt of agreement from Dan.

"I've added a box of tricks in the back of this one," he went on, nodding his head to the rear of the vehicle, "and we can talk about how to use them when we get back."

Slightly perplexed, but in truth too tired and preoccupied to take too much notice, Dan merely grunted his agreement again before voicing his concerns.

"Where the fuck did *Walter Mitty* go?" Meaning that he hadn't seen Olivier in a while.

"No idea," answered Mitch without concern, just as the red-faced Frenchman reappeared from the side of the building. He stood still, as though he didn't expect to see the two men who intimidated him so much stood up high and staring at him, before averting his eyes and scurrying past them. He didn't get far, as Ash spun around to block his path. Olivier stood still again, and Dan, fearful that he would feel persecuted told his dog to leave him.

Ash would not. He took a quick series of steps forward on his big paws and sniffed the air before dropping into a defensive pose and baring his teeth. A low but evidently threatening growl emanated from the big dog prompting Dan to snap at him louder to leave the man alone.

Olivier backed away, and when he saw that Ash would not follow he turned and walked fast.

"What's wrong with you?" he asked the dog, who had relaxed but still watched the man walking away. Ash ignored his master, and maintained visual contact with his target.

The two men stood on top of the truck looked at each other, as though both tried to figure out what that exchange had been about.

"I always said Ash was a good judge of character," Mitch said.

"Me too," agreed Dan, but almost absently. He had ignored his dog's intuition twice before, and it had almost cost him his life.

"Was it me or did he look like he'd been crying?" Dan asked the soldier.

In his reply, Mitch betrayed the very reason why he needed a commanding officer. Why, although ruthlessly effective at any task of soldiering, he worked better when the decisions were made for him. He lacked that extra layer of instinct which could turn the tide of an engagement. He merely dismissed the odd turn of events with a joke.

"Probably went for a piss and remembered how small it was!"

Dan smiled the appropriate response, but didn't let the thought dissipate with the moment. Jumping down from his perch, he called aloud for everyone to head home.

He didn't realise that the look he had seen on Olivier's face was one of shame; a look of a man ashamed of himself, ashamed of his jealousy, ashamed because his lies were uncovered. It was a look of a man who would sell his own mother for status, and it was the look of a man whose loyalty could be bought for a very low price.

⁓

The two lethal patches of undergrowth listened as the sound of four engines faded away into the distance. They stayed put, not moving an inch, until they were certain that nobody had remained behind to ambush them in the unlikely event that the little man they had captured decided to betray them. To betray his country and his army.

Slithering low to the ground they returned to the small section of fence they had cut and so painstakingly fixed back into place so as not to show any sign of their entry into the camp. Walking fast but quietly over the uneven ground they moved in silence until they regained the position of their vehicle.

Combined with the detailed activity report and carefully drawn map from his sniper, le chasseur had now obtained real-time intelligence on the strength and capabilities of his adversary. He knew the basic approach to the defence of the walled town by the sea, and, vitally, he now knew how to crack it open like an egg.

The chess pieces were forming up, and the king would fall to him.

GAME CHANGER

Waking with a gasp, sheeted with sweat and fighting to control his breathing, Steve took a few seconds to realise where he was.

He was on a folding cot, restrained by a sleeping bag, in a room with other people who all seemed blissfully unaware of the terror he had been in.

If it wasn't the reliving of the horrific events which caused him to transform from pilot in the air to a bleeding sack of meat and bone on the ground, then it was something else. More terrifying than the twisted and contorted memories and false memories of the helicopter crash, was his other recurring nightmare. The same one he had just experienced, which led him to jolt awake in such sudden fear of his own death that his body was sticky and cold as his heart pounded in his chest. In this repeating dream, he again stood on the steps of the commandeered town hall in their unhappy camp, and as he was delivering his victory speech to the grateful masses, his nemesis appeared and gunned him down. In his own nightmare, the madman he had cheated out of air superiority came to exact his terrible revenge, and the gun raised towards him in slow motion. He saw the barrel rise, was powerless to do anything about it, and stood transfixed by the black circle of the business end of the gun and waited for the flash.

That flash signalled his demise, it foretold his death, and each and every time it felt completely, utterly, and inescapably real.

Trying and failing to gain command of his breathing, his shoulders heaved and he clutched both hands to his breast bone and forced his lungs to slow their desperate race to burst.

Two whole minutes passed before he felt in any way in control of his body again, and if he hadn't known better he would have thought he was having a heart attack. He knew he wasn't, because he had experienced the same sensation over and over, at least three times each week for months now.

Slowly extricating himself from the damp sleeping bag he swung his feet out of the bed to the cold floor. In the shaft of light in front of his face beaming in from the artificial lights outside, he saw his breath mist before him. The cold December air hit his damp body then, and brought on racking shivers which made his teeth chatter involuntarily. Knowing he would not regain any sleep that night, or probably much the night after, he struggled to his feet still shivering. At least if he was done with slumber for the night then he might as well make himself more comfortable and wash away the cold layer of sweat.

Remembering to retrieve the walking stick which he hadn't needed for months, he shrugged a blanket over his shoulders and retrieved the towel and armful of clothes he had laid out for the following day; a practice he had been accustomed to for as long as he could remember, from long days at sea waiting to run to his aircraft at a moment's notice, to the days spent on intensive training where an extra minute of sleep could make all the difference. He may be damaged, crippled, and have no access to a helicopter for the remainder of his life, but he was still, at heart, a warrior.

His war had changed exponentially, and was now more akin to the French resistance of the Second World War than it was to the modern aerial warfare he had trained for and engaged in for close to three decades.

So now, remembering to appear to anyone who saw him as a broken cripple, he limped his way quietly out of the dormitory and towards the shower block.

Glancing down and squinting at the face of the watch he now wore – his own expensive diver's watch that he had worn for years had long been lost – he saw that he still had probably four hours before sunrise. With a resigned sigh, he limped onwards to the shower block.

Ever the optimist, he smiled to himself thinking that if anything good were to come of this then he would at least enjoy a piping hot shower; the reservoir tanks for the general population quickly ran cold at peak times, and a cold shower was something they all endured. He limped on under the far from watchful gaze of two guards, one of whom he strongly suspected was checking the security from behind his eyelids.

Only now he saw steam emanating from the door of the block as he approached, instantly bleeding away to nothing in the cold, dark air. Someone was enjoying the hot water he had been imagining to be all for him.

Entering the steaming and poorly lit room he allowed his eyes to adjust. The furthest shower cubicle – separated only by the lazy rigging of plastic curtains – had soapy water flowing out and into the central drain. As his eyes grew more accustomed to the steamy environment, he saw with horror that the water flowing towards his feet was laced with swathes of diluting red.

Torn between thinking he may still be asleep and fearing that he may have discovered another suicide, he dropped the stick along with his bundle of folded, dry clothes and covered the distance to the cubicle in two long strides. Tearing aside the curtain quickly, he gaped through the steam to be instantly confronted with a scream from the occupant.

Snatching at the curtain to draw it again and restore the modesty of the now terrified occupant, he slipped in the soapy water and fell heavily on his backside where he was powerless to do anything but stare up at the naked and blood-drenched form of Lizzie attempting to cover herself. She stopped mid scream, stood more upright and inadvertently flashed him an eyeful of breast, cocked her head slightly and regarded him with a questioning look.

"Steve?" she said, perplexed and relaxing as suddenly as her fear had erupted vocally.

"I'm sorry, I saw blood and I... I'm so sorry!" he blurted out like a schoolboy turning his eyes away, ashamed and embarrassed by his actions and her nakedness.

Abandoning all pretence of modesty, she stepped forwards and helped him to his feet; his embarrassed blushing thankfully hidden by the poor lighting and the steam in the air.

"A guard will have heard that, get in the shower quickly," she hissed at him, almost projecting him across the small space and into the opposite cubicle.

True enough, a guard entered ten seconds later having heard the scream. His unconcerned challenge was easily deflected, and Lizzie's easy reassurance that she had slipped but wasn't hurt satisfied the tired and bored sentry into returning to his comfortable chair where he had been dozing until she so rudely woke him.

The two showering conspirators held their collective breath until both felt that the lie had been believed. Steve stood, unsure of what to make of everything that had just happened, until the curtain twitched back in front of him and Lizzie darted in to stand beside him. Now wearing a towel wrapped around her torso, he was bizarrely more aroused at the sight of her than he had been before. Shaking his head to clear the unhelpful and inappropriate thoughts, he tuned in just in time to hear her words.

"I'm sorry," she whispered into his ear, barely audible over the sound of the shower she had left running. "You scared me and it's not like things don't happen here."

Steve's slow-moving brain was recovering speed now, and connected the dots that this is where a guard was supposed to have assaulted a woman before Richards had him publicly executed.

"I thought," he said, almost choking on his words before trying again, still unable to look directly at her for fear she would see through him. "I thought someone had hurt themselves," he finished lamely.

Suicide was a matter he suspected that many of them had considered, but hope generally held out for most people.

"It's not my blood," she said, "someone came in injured as I was leaving the hospital, and I got covered in his blood trying to save him."

Her choice of words took a few seconds to connect in Steve's brain before he asked, "Trying?"

She looked straight into his eyes, as unconcerned with her state of undress as she was the blood still in her hair.

"I tried. He didn't survive," she said blankly. Steve processed this more quickly before asking, "Us or them?" meaning was it a cog or was it one of the machine operators.

"One of them," she said, with no hint of a smile.

Steve asked what had happened, but Lizzie hushed him with placatory hand gestures. "It's not important," she interrupted. "What is important is that I report this to the resistance without getting caught."

Her revelation rocked him. He knew people knew about the resistance, obviously, but having never had the chance to speak to her in private he now realised that all his safety measures and safeguards he so painstakingly observed had worked. He had isolated the members of the movement to such an extent that the woman he knew so well had no idea that he was behind it all.

Swallowing down the first words which came to his tongue, he knew that he had to keep it that way. Another reason to do so was that a revelation had just dawned on him that, not only did he know this woman so well, but that he also harboured a deeper emotional connection to her that he hadn't fully understood until just now.

Focusing himself, he played along.

"What do you know about the resistance?" he asked.

She seemed taken aback by the question, as though she felt confident she had been imparting knowledge to the uninitiated.

"What do *you* know about it?" she shot back.

Steve fell back on his extensive training which had been innocuously called RTI, or resistance to interrogation, so many years ago.

As a military helicopter pilot, he had faced great risk of being shot down and captured by the enemy, and was trained as best he could be to survive the ordeal of being interrogated by soldiers who did not adhere to the same rules he had to. He had been taught to hold out for as long as possible, only providing the enemy with his name, rank and number, but when the risk became too great or the pain of torture became unbearable, he would fall back on half-truths and out-of-date intelligence. This was called the controlled release of information, and it was what he relied on now.

"I sometimes pass messages between people. I don't know who and I don't know what it all means. It's like a jigsaw puzzle I only have a few bits for," he lied smoothly, purely to protect them both.

Lizzie seemed impressed, as though she suddenly discovered he was a secret celebrity.

"I hear things, both from the guards and the patients, when I'm in medical. I can piece the bits together too, but what happened tonight was weird."

Steve asked how it was weird, and listened intently to her explanation.

"I was just packing up to close the clinic for the night when two guards carried in a younger one. There was so much blood I couldn't even find out where the wound was, but he'd been stabbed in the stomach. I was the only one left and I needed the doctor for emergency surgery so I sent the guards to fetch help. I tried to keep him still and stem the bleeding but I had no chance of stopping it without surgery." She paused, looking down as though she was reliving the story and not simply recounting it. Steve reached up and placed a hand on her shoulder, happy to wait for her to be ready to tell the remainder of the tale.

"He kept trying to push my hands away from the wound, kept saying 'Will'…" She swallowed, now totally immersed in the memory. Steve couldn't be sure if the water running down her cheeks was from her wet hair or tears from her eyes.

"He told me that another one of *them* did it, and they wouldn't stop until they had finished the job."

Pausing again, Steve gave her shoulder a gentle squeeze of encouragement. She raised her face, looked directly into his eyes and delivered the biggest, most important single piece of intelligence his resistance movement had ever gleaned.

"He died in my arms, but before he went he told me they're planning to take over the camp," she said with savage finality.

Steve's face showed the appropriate level of shock, but inside his brain went off like a firework display. Will? The twins? Seizing control from Richards? Murdering their own?

This threw so many things out of orbit that he had been completely unaware of and shattered his plan for a mostly peaceful takeover. A rogue element of guards led by the savage brothers was not a fly this particular ointment could endure, and he had to re-evaluate quickly.

"I can get this to the resistance," he told her, seeing the relief and emotion wash over her face as she now unburdened herself of the terrible experience she had just been put through. She seemed to deflate, her eyes showing sadness as her chin quivered. She let go of her strong exterior and cried, burying her face deep in his neck and sobbing. He just stood there, holding the half-naked and soaking wet nurse who had saved his leg and his life. The woman he was attracted to, yet no amount of lust could make him consider taking advantage of her vulnerability. She was part of his resistance, whether she knew it was his or not, and she was willing to risk her life to get the information to those who could act on it.

Finally, her crying abated and she wordlessly returned to her shower to rinse the last of the red from her pale hair. She dried herself, dressed, and left the block, all without saying another word. Steve retrieved his wet clothes, decided they would probably dry after he had worn them for a while, and stripped down to wash away the sticky residue of his nightmare.

Shivering under the tepid drizzle, Lizzie's extended shower having obliterated the chance of the hot water he had been anticipating, he steeled himself for a fight far bigger than he had thought was on the horizon, and that horizon was looming fast.

Max flinched in his chair in the grand hallway as whatever had been thrown inside Richards's office hit the wall with a resounding thud. He sat still and listened, staring resolutely ahead and trying his hardest to look like he knew nothing; he did, mostly, but he was certain that his dishonesty was tattooed on his forehead.

Despite the thick walls and heavy wooden door, he could clearly make out every word being screamed inside. The tirade had gone on for more than ten minutes already, having begun shortly after he had summoned the highest echelons of the leadership before their breakfast. Currently inside the room being roasted by the Major were the two brothers, both wearing stone-cold expressions of blankness, and three deputy commanders responsible for the daily running of the camp.

Having received no orders to enter the grand office and takes notes, Max had returned to his desk and sat in fearful silence until his over-inflated receptionist duties were required once more.

"I will ask you again, *gentlemen*," Richards shouted with acidic emphasis. "How exactly did this happen?"

Max heard one of the men clear his throat and begin to spout meaningless waffle about being understaffed, and that they couldn't possibly double every guard duty before the voice trailed away suddenly as another missile was launched against the wall, this one shattering to play a decorative tinkling sound as the broken pieces of what Max guessed was a crystal decanter exploded.

Nobody filled the silence, and Richards carried on. "You two are oddly quiet," he snarled threateningly, and Max imagined the two unnaturally and intrinsically linked brothers shooting a brief glance at each other, seemingly communicating telepathically.

"Isolated incident, sir," one of them replied woodenly.

"From what our sources say, the man was overly friendly with some of the workers—" this from one of the others who was eager to interject with something helpful before Richards destroyed his attempts to ingratiate himself.

"I was asking an organ-grinder, not a monkey. Speak when addressed directly, sir," the Major spat with his own specific brand of well-mannered abuse, silencing the man instantly. Max allowed himself a smirk as he pictured the jowly face of the man nominally in charge of organising the working parties outside of the camp turning crimson with impotent rage and shame.

"Isolated incident? Elucidate," Richards commanded.

Max could only hear a few words of the explanation, which he guessed came from the older brother who had a quieter, yet infinitely more frightening, voice. From what he could glean without moving or pressing his ear to the wall for fear of being discovered, he thought that the brothers were painting a picture of a guard who had become inappropriately close to a number of people he was guarding. Their best joint assessment was that the man had become embroiled in something and had ultimately fetched himself a knife to the guts for his involvement.

That reasonable, yet simplistic, report seemed to satisfy Richards. Max knew he liked a simple solution presented to him, as he had to merely give the idea his blessing as opposed to actively think about anything other than his current mad-hat idea. His last one was to instruct Max to find someone among the population who could paint his likeness and immortalise him in oil and canvas.

Max listened to the summary from the brothers as they bounced from each other like an endless tennis rally, speaking as though one person's lines were being recited by two actors auditioning for the same role. Their easy assumption and confident report that the man only had himself to blame only made the report Max clutched in his hand all the more important. And all the more believable.

Eventually Richards's rage abated and he gave orders before dismissing the assembled men. He believed he gave orders, but Max knew by being the silent middle man that those orders were taken by a number of the senior ranks as mere suggestions. A few made minor alterations to their orders, all under the guise of real-time streamlining or tactical readjustments or whatever they wrote on their reports to justify the fact that they had a better way of doing things than Richards had suggested. The brothers were the worst; they didn't even pretend to try and follow orders, but simply deployed guards where they saw fit and often ignored their instructions entirely. Which is why, after hearing their assertions about the death of the guard, he knew for certain that the anonymous intelligence submission held in his hand and deposited on his desk late last night was absolutely true. The note simply read:

I have been asked to join a group to overthrow the Major. I'm meeting with the brothers tonight and will report back in the morning.

At first glance Max hadn't known what to do with this information, but whilst he was still ruminating a blood-soaked doctor appeared at the door with two others flanking him. He had reported the murder of a guard directly to Richards and suffered a barrage of abuse for not raising the alarm immediately. Max had then been ordered to assemble his senior officers and at no time did he have the opportunity to speak in confidence and warn the Major of the treachery.

Nor did he think that would do any good. The Major was, without a doubt, insane. He hid it well but Max had no confidence in his ability to cope with this news rationally, and feared it would be turned on him as the bearer of bad news. So now he sat and clutched the scrap of paper as though he could squeeze a sensible answer out of it.

He sat for a long time thinking. He had to deal with the interruption of Richards giving a string of orders to be written, copied into the occurrence book Max was forced to keep in a neat hand, and when he hesitated Richards pounced on the indecisiveness as insubordination. Max instantly apologised and assured the Major that he would never disobey his orders, but that he was in shock at the murder of the guard. He did his best to look vulnerable and upset, correctly assuming that Richards would then soften and offer magnanimous fatherly advice on how to cope with losses in conflict. Max lapped it up, thanked the Major for his patience and kind words, then went to work.

He kept that piece of paper hidden all day until the conclusion of his duties, then quietly knocked on the door of the big office.

"Come," came the crisp reply. He entered to find Richards busily writing in a leather-bound ledger, doubtlessly recording the latest chapter in his memoirs which would immortalise the saviour of the human race long after his passing.

"Sir, with your permission I'd like to visit my family tonight," he said respectfully. He had no family, but Richards was not to know that the few people he had been captured with – or *rescued* with as he had to refer to it –were unrelated.

Richards made a show of steepling his fingers and leaning back to think as he gestured for Max to sit opposite him. Silently he rose and poured two measures of scotch from the newly acquired replacement decanter.

"Of course, Max. Of course," he said as he sat in the leather chair next to his assistant and offered a glass to him. "It's important to remember who we are fighting this war for. Go and be with your family, but remember to be back inside HQ by curfew."

The curfew had been reinstated that day given the previous night's incident, but Max would be one of the few 'civilians' who could still walk around unchallenged due to Richards's unnerving personal interest in him.

"I mean what I say, Max," Richards said intensely as he leaned across and placed a hand on his knee. Max tried his hardest not to flinch or recoil and give offence. He hated scotch and suspected that Richards had already sipped a few glasses that afternoon. To give a natural pause to the awkward moment Max drained his glass and leaned forward to place the empty crystal tumbler on the desk, subtly dislodging Richards's hand as he moved.

"I will, sir, I promise," he said with a smile as though he truly appreciated the man's concern for his safety.

Walking from the office slowly he closed the door and checked to see that nobody else was in the hallway before he allowed his body to shudder from head to toe. Shaking himself out of the moment he strode purposefully from the big building and down the wide stone steps, nodding as he went to the two men manning the sandbagged positions permanently in place to protect the inner sanctum of the regime.

Walking slowly with his head down so as not to attract any attention, he aimed for the main dining area. He had no idea how or where he would make contact, but he had to find the man which all the intelligence reports alluded to. The man Richards had been obsessed with but had now forgotten. The man he suspected was at the centre of some kind of underground resistance movement.

Queuing with the others for his meal, feeling like a traitor as his own food was of far better quality than what was being served to the general population, he glanced around to try and find the man he hoped could help them all.

ERROR 404 – SLEEP NOT FOUND

"I told you I don't know what you're talking about," Lexi said, her words sounding slow and sluggish.

"What is sanctuary?" growled her interrogator again, repeating himself in the same menacingly patient monotone as though she hadn't spoken.

Unable to form another reply, Lexi just shook her head from side to side, her movements unnatural and forced with none of the poise and grace she had previously possessed. She didn't even know if the man spoke English other than the three questions he asked repeatedly.

"What is sanctuary?" growled the man again, uncaring as to any answer he may or may not receive.

Unable to respond with anything that would please her captors, Lexi's head slumped and her vision flashed white. She didn't know if she had been struck - although they hadn't physically hurt her since they were first captured - or whether she was experiencing another painful blackout as she had a few times over the last weeks. Or days, or hours. She had no way to know for certain.

The flash extended to become bright lights, and then she realised that the fluorescent tubes on the ceiling above her were illuminated, mesmerising her with the almost imperceptible flickering and pulsing. She knew now that they had moved her again, as the last room was the one with the pipes and a single bulb.

They did this; kept moving her between rooms and never allowing her to sleep comfortably. One of the rooms even had a bed in it, but her bound hands were tied to a fixing in the wall which prevented her from reaching it. She sat forlornly next to the bed and cried until she ran out of tears.

But that was weeks ago, she thought, *wasn't it?*

The man was gone, she realised, but it took her a while to get her bearings in preparation for another interrogator to come through the door at any moment.

What is sanctuary?

Where are you from?

What are you doing here?

Three simple questions with such a multitude of different answers depending on the wants and needs of her captors.

The way he had said 'sanctuary' made Lexi think that it was a place and not a concept. So, in that sense, she didn't know.

She had told them time and again that she had come from England. They had driven here. When these answers failed to satisfy, her ramblings continued to describe the home she had grown up in as a child. About the garden and the swing set her father had put together for her seventh birthday which she fell off and scraped her knee and shin painfully. About the school she had attended. About the boy who had kissed her for a dare when she was ten years old and had then run to his friends to mock her.

It seemed that this previously unrecalled depth and clarity also failed to satisfy the interrogator, so her addled brain wandered off elsewhere.

What was she doing there? In her more lucid moments she knew she was there because the four of them failed. They had simply wandered up to strangers and said hello, not recognising the obvious likelihood of them being unfriendly. She was there because they had kidnapped her and at least one of the others, that she knew of, based on her logical assumptions from the sounds of screaming, and now they asked her the same questions every day.

She retreated into her mind once more, recalling with startling accuracy a televised documentary on the use of sleep deprivation as a weapon of torture. The words of the narrator came to her, only in the ruins of her imagination the narrator was a large, colourful parrot which eyed her suspiciously as it bobbed its head in time with the words.

"The use of sleep deprivation is not a new concept; in fact, the earliest documented research of sleep deprivation was recorded in the late 1800s in Russia..."

Her face twitched involuntarily, making the narrating parrot flap its wings and shift position to caw at her before it resumed its own interruption.

"...little has changed in modern use for interrogation and psychological warfare. Symptoms on the body can include irritability, severe mood swings, impaired cognitive and emotional abilities and responses as well as more obvious physiological reactions; muscle spasms, poor coordination, tremors and painful aches..."

Lexi tilted her head in mimic of the parrot who waddled closer to regard her with its tilted head fixing her with a single, black beady eye.

"...long terms effects are uncertain, but an increased risk of heart disease and diabetes is as likely as premature death…"

"I wish," Lexi said aloud in a groggy voice. The door banged open and the parrot glanced back at the noise. Lexi saw a man walk in and close the door behind him, the shadowy light in the doorway making her guess that it was some time in the morning. Or maybe the early afternoon. When she looked back the parrot was gone, abandoning her like everyone else in her life had. The man walked to her and silently thrust a water bottle under her nose with a sports cap on the top. No longer caring enough to be suspicious, Lexi sucked on the bottle thirstily until it was taken away from her. Gasping after the sudden effort, she sat back to catch her breath.

The man leaned down to look her in the eye for a while before speaking.

"What is Sanctuary?" he said quietly.

Hundreds of miles north of Lexi's tomb, someone else was struggling with the effects of sleep deprivation, although by no means to the same extent.

His symptoms were irritability and blurred vision when his focus wavered. He ached and he had a dull headache which he feared would never go away. His older brother, annoyingly more alert but infinitely more worried startled him by approaching from the shadows – something that would never have happened if he had his senses on full alert. The two had not slept the previous night, so had in effect been awake for nearing forty hours straight. Not only that, those forty hours had been packed full of action, stress, fear and pretending.

They – or more specifically he, the impetuous Will – had judged one of their recruits poorly. Very poorly. They had a dozen guards, men of ability and ambition, securely attached to their cause now. Discovery would mean death as a traitor so they picked carefully, with one exception. The meeting had gone smoothly, but one recruit was very twitchy and kept asking questions. The man wanted specifics; times, locations, numbers. He sealed his own fate by overtly asking for the detailed information which would be used to formulate a report on the abilities and intentions of the rebels. He was so obvious that even he realised it, too late. At once the others around the small fire moved and penned the man into a corner of the shed they were in. He drew a knife and stood, terrified, holding his impossible defence against the others.

That was when Benjamin first stepped up to offer his opinion on the matter. If Will was the hot-headed one of the two, then Benjamin more than made up for that with his almost eerie self-control. There was no other way to describe it; he was just plain *cold*.

Stepping through the semi-circle of men fearful of the primal power of a blade, he calmly walked to within striking distance of the shaking man and stood still with his arms at his sides. He stared long into his eyes; cold calculation meeting terrified desperation. He smiled.

"Who else knows?" he asked calmly.

The man holding the quivering knife swallowed, his Adam's apple bobbing up and down in his throat with excessive exaggeration. He said nothing.

"Who else knows?" Benjamin said again, injecting the slightest hint of threat and steel into the question.

The Adam's apple rose and fell quickly once more, but no words came.

Fractionally moving his right foot, Benjamin caused the scratch of gravel under his boot sole to make everyone assembled jump with sudden fright. The man holding the knife spasmed, barely managing to control himself and not attack out of sheer panic. He held his blade, still wavering, pointing at the unmoving chest of Benjamin, who just smiled in response to the threat.

The man's nerve broke and he lunged.

Benjamin anticipated the attack; he knew with absolute certainty that having placed his body where he had, the man would lunge for the closest target he presented. Shooting the sharp blade out in a straight stab, the man let out a yell of combined fear and rage.

Benjamin let the knife come to him, turning his body slightly by swinging his right shoulder forward and allowing the movement to dictate the flow of the rest of his upper body. Swinging inwards like a revolving door, he brought his right hand up and slapped his palm into the wrist of the hand holding the blade and gripped. Simultaneously he slapped the palm of his left hand on the back of his attacker's outstretched grip, the tense ligaments feeling raised and taught as he pressed it upwards and out.

The combined movement of both hands had the instant effect of destroying the strength of the man's grip on the knife and turning the hand inwards so the knife now pointed inwards, still towards Benjamin, only now without the strength and momentum he had before.

Out of the desperate instinct to survive, the attacker did not give up just because his first attack was deflected; he still had the weapon and needed only to push it a matter of inches into the chest of

Benjamin. Switching his footing clumsily, he renewed the power behind the thrust and yelled harder as he went for the kill.

The yell wavered and changed pitch, turning instead to a higher note of fear. Instant and utter fear at his own imminent death.

Instead of the knife burying its blade between the ribs of Benjamin, the man felt the impetus of his attack keep turning and swing, taking him off balance. In horror he watched on as his own hand holding the knife was turned inwards with ease, as though no matter how hard he tried the mechanics simply were possible, and the sweeping movement continued as the knife safely bypassed the body of Benjamin and headed, interminably and terribly, back towards his own body.

The yell stopped abruptly with a strangled cry and he felt that all the breath was sucked out of him. He couldn't breathe, and the pain was utterly consuming.

"Did you tell anyone?" Benjamin hissed in his ear, close as a lover.

It was the most painful, horrendous thing the man had ever experienced, and he seemed unable to draw breath for minutes. He just managed to make eye contact with Benjamin and shake his head; this final lie his only possible act of defiance.

Looking down, cradling the knife softly with his own bloody hands, he finally took a breath and filled his lungs. The split second before he released that breath in an earth-shattering scream, Benjamin lashed out like a viper and struck him once, impossibly hard, in the windpipe and silenced him instantly.

Falling back against the wall, his body awash with fiery pain, he slumped towards the ground. He couldn't tell which was worse; the feeling of suffocating or the knife deep in his belly that welled out piping-hot blood in big gushes.

He knew the others were talking, but he couldn't make out the words. Benjamin was giving orders, pointing at people, and he was vaguely aware of two of the others hauling him up uncaringly and carrying him away. The cold night air stung him as he jolted around in paralysed agony, looking up and seeing the occasional weak light in the black sky which showed his hot breath misting.

His last memory was being thumped down on the cold, hard table and a woman looking down on him, asking his name.

If he had been able, he would've told her that he was called Jason. That he had tried to do the right thing. That he had failed. That he was sorry. He managed to utter a few words and watched as her eyes grew wide.

He died, although he had been in so much pain that death was a welcome relief.

Now, meeting his brother in the cold and dark, Will wanted to apologise for his poor choice in recruit. Opening his mouth to start, he was silenced by Benjamin speaking first.

"I think he told us the truth," he said quietly. "If he had told someone, then we wouldn't have been trusted to give out orders today. If he'd told Richards we'd have been up against the wall wearing a blindfold at first light."

Will thought on this, seeing no obvious holes in the story presented to him. He didn't think for long; his brother was the born tactician whereas he just enjoyed the violence.

"So what do we do now?" he asked his older brother.

"Stick to the plan," Benjamin replied. "We take over and kill any fucker who gets in the way."

INVINCIBILITY LIES IN THE DEFENCE

The sun was setting by the time the convoy returned to the gates of Sanctuary. They were met by Leah, Polly and Marie with little ceremony. Mitch, as ever, showing no signs of weariness but only excitement at their haul, was disappointed not to be asked to work through the night. Instead, Dan ordered all arms and munitions unloaded into a heavy stone room without windows by the gatehouse. Polly, in between carrying boxes and catching her breath, told Dan that he was probably the first man in a hundred years to order the magazine stocked. Dan knew precisely what she meant, but allowed the explanation to be heard by all the others.

The windowless circular room with impossibly thick, stone walls and a heavy wooden door was the powder magazine for the gatehouse and would have served the cannon defending the approach. There was no better place to store the arms they had recovered, either practically or metaphorically.

Instructing everyone to get some food and rest, thanking them for their efforts, he asked for three volunteers to remove the vehicles from blocking the gatehouse and walk back; the return journey they had made that morning.

Leah offered herself, obviously itching to get outside where she could find some form of danger to prove herself against. Dan asked her instead to take Ash and feed him. Any normal teenager may have argued with him, or at least made her displeasure well known, but Leah simply regarded his expression for a second before deciding that he clearly had other 'volunteers' in mind for a reason. Walking away with a small nod she patted his body armour affectionately as she passed, clicking her fingers for the dog's attention.

Scanning the group, his eyes rested on Olivier. His fixed gaze, conveying no malice but simple expectation, gained the result he wanted.

"I will go," he said, with obvious reluctance.

Two others volunteered themselves, a man and woman who appeared to be a couple. Mitch caught Dan's eye and shot him a look of concern. Dan knew what he meant, but wouldn't entertain a warning of going outside at night with three of 'them' and none of 'us' to back him up. Not even his dog.

Dan intended this, partly to offer a display of vulnerability to his allies, but mostly to show that he trusted them. He wasn't one to accept the offer of a bodyguard on a bad day, let alone now.

A guard was placed on the door, Adam teaming up with a young Frenchman and trying to communicate with a bizarre hybrid of speaking slowly and pointing, to keep the newly amassed arsenal safe from causal interest. As he prepared to leave, Dan noticed that Mitch took a significantly larger bag to his room than he had brought with him that morning.

Kid in a sweet shop, he thought to himself with a smile.

Leading his small group back to the large hanger-type building where the vehicles were to be stored, Dan drove the awkward and ungainly French military transport truck, it's six wheels making easy but slow progress on the rutted tracks which used to be roads. Checking his mirrors to ensure that three sets of sidelights were snaking along behind him, Dan's attention was grabbed by the dials and switches on the upper section of the cab. Never having been a radio expert, he ignored its presence and concentrated on the road as he reminded himself to ask someone smarter than himself to check it out.

The vehicles were stored without any fuss and in relative silence, and the careful walk back in the dark began. Luckily the moon was high and bright, shooting a wavering line along the rippling water out to sea. Dan wished he could have had Ash with him, his superhero level sense of smell and hearing always reassured Dan in the dark, but he knew with absolute certainty that the dog would not allow Olivier close enough to him without inspiring fear in the diminutive Frenchman, so he had insisted he stayed behind.

Now, feeling slightly under-equipped, Olivier made his move.

"We did a good job today, no?" he asked in English, the flash of white teeth reflecting the moonlight betraying the faked smile he wore.

"We did very well," Dan agreed, speaking slowly to assist his understanding; too often he was accused of mumbling and didn't want the language barrier to be worsened for this conversation.

A silence hung for a dozen strides, their footfalls in sync but with Olivier taking uncomfortably longer paces to match the taller Englishman. Dan kept this pace intentionally, forcing a subconscious superiority on the man.

"Have you been to war, Olivier?" Dan asked simply.

A pause of three paces, before he replied, "Yes and no."

"Meaning you went to war but never fought?" Dan enquired, prompting another three step delay.

"Yes," he said, shame and embarrassment heavy in his voice.

Dan let the answer swirl around his head, as though savouring an expensive drink in his mouth. Behind him he could hear the muffled conversation between the others.

"Why did you tell people you were a soldier?" Dan asked him, again the simplicity of his questions carried the brutality of truth. Olivier wanted to protest, to say that he *had* been a soldier, even if he lied about having seen action. His shame stung his eyes, and he realised that he had thought so long he had forgotten to answer.

"To be more…" he struggled over the word, "…better?" he tried.

"To look good to the others?" Dan asked, keeping his rising anger in check more easily than he had expected given Olivier's disarming honesty.

"Yes," came the simple answer.

Dan paused, maintaining his pace which Olivier had to take extra skipping steps to match.

"You won't be guarding the gate any more. You'll be putting everyone in danger," Dan said. It wasn't a question, or even an instruction. He was simply stating fact. He expected Olivier to argue, but instead the man surprised him.

"Send me to the fort. I can be better there," he pleaded.

Dan suspected he meant that he could be useful as another defender in the sky fort, and that would also mean that Dan would barely see the man as the stone steps were not something anyone wanted to take as a daily commute. He hadn't thought of this as an option, but he saw no downsides to the suggestion.

"I'll think about it," he said, allowing the smaller man to drop behind and walk at a more sustainable pace.

Guessing he was maybe twenty metres out in front, Dan muttered to himself, "If you have any balls, little man, now is the time to shoot me in the back."

No shot came, instead the ground dropped away steeply into the approach to Sanctuary, where he walked through the gates, climbed the steps and slept soundly in his own bed.

The night's sleep was short, as most people were eager to see the results of the previous day's efforts. So many people were milling around to see what exciting treats were in store that Dan had to hand pick a team to help and send everyone else away as politely as possible.

Mitch went to work sorting and storing the HK416 assault rifles, creating stockpiles of different parts and interchangeable barrels. As he worked, he kept small sections clear for what seemed to be a personal project. Any interruption to his thought process was greeted by grunts and a dismissive wave, usually followed by some swearing.

Dan organised one of the .50cal heavy machine guns to be carried up the spiral stairs to the walkway above the gate, taking three people to safely manhandle the beast of a gun without damaging it. Neil, flanked by what seemed to be his French counterpart and understudy, sorted out the necessary tools and fixings they would need to secure the thing in place and hope that it didn't shake itself loose. He said as much to Neil, who returned a big grin in his direction.

"Remember Thunderbird 2?" he said.

"How could I forget?!" Dan answered, and, how could he? The big machine gun – although still far smaller than the ones they now had in their possession – had been mounted into the back of a Land Rover and used twice to devastating and deadly effect.

"Rubber mounts," Neil declared, oblivious to the fact that nobody had subtitles to his thought process. "Mike developed them, remember? They took the shaking and absorbed it so the fixings weren't ripped out of the metal."

"Rubber mounts," Dan agreed before adding, "Scotty, make it so." and walking away to leave this project in Neil's capable hands.

Ignoring the fact that Dan had murdered two Star Trek references into one, Neil shouted a reply to his friend's back.

"Ah cannae do it, Captain! She does'ne have the *power*!" he called in his best Scottish approximation.

Smiling, Dan skipped down the stone steps with ease, almost colliding with Leah at the base.

She was heavily laden with two large skeletal rifles, almost as big as she had been when he first found her, and a bag which the sight of the straining strap over her slim shoulder made Dan guess was loaded with ammunition.

The rifles were the HK417, so the ammunition would have to be the heavier 7.62 than the rounds she carried for her M4. Her own vest would be unlikely to stop two of these projectiles, but he didn't think she needed to know; not to protect her youthful innocence, but more that he was certain she knew the capability of the rounds used, having fired them at people herself with lethal effect.

"Who are we putting in the tower?" she asked, evidently having allocated herself as the person organising snipers.

"No idea yet," Dan answered honestly; the best shots he knew at distance were himself, Mitch and Leah and he knew he couldn't do without any of them for an extended period. "Someone local if they can shoot well enough and stay awake."

"Roger," she said, turning and walking away, no doubt to seek out someone qualified. Continuing down to the makeshift armoury he was greeted by a kneeling Mitch holding out a gleaming new rifle to him under a big smile.

"To replace the one you lost," he announced simply before adding with a smirk, "not that you could hit a barn door with it."

Dan ignored the goading slight, mostly as he knew it was complete rubbish, and regarded the gun offered to him as he took it.

To him, although this would probably have been a very strange concept to anyone from their old lives, it was beautiful. The shortened 10-inch barrel sprouted a fat suppressor from the end, whilst an angled grip sat neatly underneath with a torch mounted on the left side. Dan felt with his left hand and saw that Mitch had placed it just right so his left thumb could flick up to engage the powerful LED beam. On the top sat a similar configuration to his old gun, in that a small telescopic sight could be flipped to the side to reveal a clear optic with a single red dot in the middle, enabling him to shoot both at mid-range and up close and personal. The short barrel meant it could be used in confined spaces where he would normally have had to resort to his sidearm or the brutal shotgun.

Turning it over in his hands, marvelling at the lightweight yet balanced feel of the gun, he looked back to Mitch with genuine thanks. Lost for words, he merely nodded his satisfaction which pleased the soldier.

"This bugger's mine!" Mitch said with relish, climbing to his feet and lifting a longer version of the gun up for inspection. It was almost identical to Dan's, although the added few inches of barrel made the gun look far more deadly somehow but the item that caught Dan's attention was there in place of the angled foregrip of his own. It was a different shade of black metal, and somehow looked older than the rest of the gun, but its purpose was unmistakable.

"Expecting trouble, *Herr Schwarzenegger*?" Dan asked him with raised eyebrows.

"Oh!" Mitch said in mock indignation clutching one hand to his chest as though Dan had wounded him. "You think my new grenade launcher is excessive?"

They both laughed and Dan slapped a hand onto the man's shoulder with an accompanying good-natured insult. If anyone knew how best to use their limited supply of the small, flying bombs that thing could fire, then he had the utmost faith in Mitch's abilities. He had never fired one personally, or even seen one fired for that matter, but he knew enough to realise that the destructive power of that one man's rifle alone would be devastating.

"Just you!" Dan said, making it clear that he didn't want just anyone lobbing 40mm grenades around the town.

"Yes boss," Mitch answered, turning back to his duties of sorting out the remainder of the armoury and preparing to equip a militia if and when the need arose.

Turning away he had that familiar feeling of having set the wheels of a plan in motion and now found himself at a loss for gainful employment. Everyone was working, doing the tasks he had delegated under specific supervision, and now he was not immediately required. As he always did in these moments, he found somewhere to light a cigarette and take a brief pause to fill the time. Wandering back up the stone steps he saw that the mounting of the huge machine gun was well underway and needed no input from him, so he stood a way off and enjoyed the solitary smoke as Neil encouraged, cajoled and generally yelled and pointed his way through the process. Dan had yet to fix a sling for his new weapon, so he rested it, barrel pointing upwards, against the stone wall as he watched Neil's team drill holes in the ancient stone and carefully pour in a concrete mix to embed the heavy metal mounts. Dan knew he would then somehow attach the thick rubber mounts he spoke of to cushion the violent vibration of the big gun, and that would serve to keep it safely in place.

Taking a final drag and squeezing the filter of his unfamiliar tasting French cigarette between thumb and forefinger before flicking away over the wall, he turned and saw Marie approaching, flanked by a few others including Kate and Polly. The former watched his pregnant woman out of the corner of her eye, wary of the uneven footing and her delicate condition, and the latter smiled at something Neil was shouting in an appalling French accent which sounded more like an impression than a literal translation.

"Report!" Marie barked at the father of her unborn child in mockery of his old, old life. Catching on to the joke immediately, Dan snapped to attention.

"Ma'am," he said, snapping off a crisp salute with his eyes facing resolutely forward. "Gun emplacement underway, small arms are being organised and sniper arrangement for the watchtower has been delegated to junior ranks. Ma'am," he finished, relaxing to the collection of amused grins at the couple's interaction.

The matriarchal parade had collective faith in Dan and the others to organise the specifics of their defence, but the unsaid fact remained that no fighter is effective for more than a few hours without a support network. Dan mused on this to himself as the others talked, half listening to them, and tried to recall the statistics he had been taught so many years ago. It was something along the lines of; having one fighting soldier at the front line required ten others in supporting roles. That fighter had to be fed, had to be armed and equipped, had to have somewhere to be fixed up if he was hurt, had to have someone able to organise getting him home if needed, had to have people maintaining the radio sets he relied upon for real time information, and needed others to provide that up to date intelligence. Something he thought of stung a memory he couldn't quite place – couldn't recall if it was something in his subconscious from before or after the fall of the modern world. Just as quickly, he was snapped out of his reverie by the sound of his name.

"Sorry?" he said, looking at the assembled faces all staring at him.

"I asked if you had chance to speak to Olivier?" Polly enquired again, a placatory look of hope on her face.

"Yes," Dan answered, the conversation from the previous night returning to him easily, "and I've agreed he can move up to the fort as he's asked. I haven't told him yet." He looked around, for the first time mindful that he hadn't seen the man since they had returned by moonlight the previous night.

The response seemed to satisfy Polly, who exchanged a brief look with Marie. No doubt the two women had already discussed this, and he suspected, had he not provided the correct answer, then he assumed he would have had his mind changed for him.

Leah reappeared without her previous burden of heavy weaponry, and Dan waved her over to spare him having to talk to too many people – the thought still lingered at the back of his mind and knew it would stay there, lurking, if he couldn't concentrate on whatever it was that had nudged his subconscious.

"Leah, you might want to ask Polly about the personnel you need," he said, waiting for the penny to drop and then walking away with a gentle touch of Marie's elbow as the teenager launched into her requirements for a vigilant person who could shoot a rifle.

Marie walked with him and, a few paces away from the conversation, turned to face her.

"How are you feeling now?" he asked, as the last time he had seen her this morning was when she was repelling her breakfast.

"Better," she said, "hungry now though! I thought the bloody morning sickness was supposed to pass?"

Dan had no answer for that; Marie had suffered daily from shortly after they had arrived at Sanctuary and the morning routine of vomiting hadn't abated since. She was maybe eight weeks away from giving birth and now the medication she was being given didn't help things. The blood thinners caused her to feel nauseous and dizzy, and combined with livid bruising from the slightest of knocks, she also suffered from bleeding gums every time she cleaned her teeth. She often joked about him loving her even though she looked awful, and he would always deftly deflect her goading. As a result of her frailty, Kate took it upon herself to either watch her personally, or have someone with her at all times. Their erstwhile paramedic was initially against the theory of using such aggressive medication on an otherwise healthy woman, even more so that she was pregnant, but eventually agreed that it was the only course of action available given the circumstances. She had studied the results of the town's only woman to have had a baby born alive, and agreed that, although unorthodox, there was no other way to ensure Marie and Dan's baby survived.

Dan knew that Marie was putting on a brave exterior, but deeper down he knew that, more than the sickness, she felt impotent and useless. She was weak, she tired easily, and she suffered bouts of confusion which dulled her sharpest weapon; her intellect. Finally, and reluctantly, she allowed herself to be cared for and although Dan's absence sometimes upset her, she knew that he was doing what he did best to ensure her – and their baby's – survival.

"Rest, please," he said to her, giving her a kiss on the cheek and feeling the warmth of her skin as she leaned into him. Glancing up over her shoulder he saw Kate watching their embrace, and nodded slightly to her, signalling that he felt Marie had enjoyed enough fresh air. Watching on as Kate led her away, he chalked up another thing, correction *things*, to worry about on top of their defence and long term survival.

Returning to Leah to see her deep in discussion with Polly he felt another surge of emotion, this time fatherly admiration more than worry. Leah first came into his life as a naïve, sarcastic and frightened young girl. After almost two years she was still a sarcastic young girl, but she had metamorphosed into something so unique: terrible yet brilliant, frightening but caring. He thought back over the years he had spent fighting alongside others, and the time he had spent fighting crime with various partners, and wished that on any single day he could've had the young girl as his backup. True, her childhood had come to an abrupt end, and he was a likely cause of that by removing her youthful innocence and replacing it with a gun and the training to use it properly, but he didn't force it on her.

She was an evolution.

An adaptation.

A demonstration of the human ability to react to circumstance and prosper. She was the caterpillar emerging from a chrysalis to spread her wings, but instead she came out armed and smiling.

None of this could he have articulated, and to simply say that he loved the girl was woefully insufficient. He respected her, cared for her in many fatherly ways but treated her in most senses as an equal. Now, watching as she walked away with the effective mayor of the town, he saw and heard how a child deftly moulded the conversation without seeming manipulative. That, he was certain, he hadn't taught her.

He felt no need to oversee that task; Leah would pick someone appropriate to accompany the old man high on the hill, taking into account their personality and ability alongside their nature so as not to clash. In short, she would, he knew, try to find the old man a friend and betray the fact that there was still a sweet young girl in there.

Dan's attention was snatched away by Neil slapping him hard on the backside, making Ash skitter away unsure of what had happened, before he recalled he had a reputation to uphold, and adopted a more menacing look towards the man who had startled him.

"Let that set for a bit," he said before Dan could offer an opinion on his stinging buttock, meaning the fixings he had just concreted into place. "Next one lads!" he announced, waving his entourage to the stairs to fetch the other heavy gun and carry it the back-breaking distance to the seaward defences. Dan accompanied them, doing his bit by slinging his new gun and hauling a heavy metal container of huge linked ammunition in each hand. He had to stop every fifty paces or so and shake his arms to get the blood flow vaguely back to normal before resuming. His slow progress wasn't an issue, as the already-tired crew carrying the gun and the heavy tripod were making slower progress. After they had crossed over the small bridge spanning the water's widening path to the protected bay, Dan saw Mitch's new 'friend' approaching with a small trolley. He guessed from having seen similar things on holidays, that this was the cart she used to transport heavy compressed air diving tanks from her shop to the sea, and having seen their plight had emptied it and now came to offer her help. Hiding behind her hair, she merely wheeled it into the path of the machine gun team and stopped there, waiting for them to mutely understand. A sweating Neil was effusive in his thanks, maybe a little over the top if Dan had to be honest, and the gun was loaded. He found space to stack his ammo boxes, as did the others carrying similar burdens, and added his own body weight to the combined effort of pushing the cart along the cobbled street.

Reaching the foot of the raised sea wall which led to the low, circular stone watch tower he left the team to their task and returned at a more relaxed pace to the gatehouse. He had discussed the sea-facing defences with Neil, and as the older man had already found himself on that side of town as some crazy foreign inventor and all-round tinkerer of things, he had agreed to remain as the de facto commander of that gun battery. He would have to leave Mitch in charge of the gate gun, which would leave himself and Leah to command the remainder of the militia to wherever they were needed in the event of an attack.

The plan was basic, but it had to be. They were truly dealing with a militia, a civilian army, and their tasks had to be simple. A professional soldier could be expected to multitask; to switch between firing mortars and having to man a heavy machine gun to include clearing jams and swapping barrels in quick time but a militia could not. Dan's imagination treated their forces, although not unkindly, as the peasantry who would herd their livestock inside the walls and join the defence with their pitchforks.

Keep it simple, stupid.

Groups of people would be trained to use the big guns, but not through live-firing exercises as they were literally firing a quickly exhausted supply. Bullets were, as of almost two years ago, an endangered species.

The question of the anti-tank rockets, the disposable 'fire and forget' things was raised, and it was agreed that asking a civilian to use one of those would be somewhere between unfair and catastrophically dangerous. Best keep those particular ace cards up their collective sleeves.

Standing on the upper ramparts once again, reunited with his new toy and accompanied by his dog, he scanned an all-round view of the town and imagined them now to be a damned hard target.

SUSPICION

Steve watched subtly from his quiet corner of the dining hall. He had worked hard to become all but invisible over the last few months, but within minutes of the unfamiliar face walking into the room the whisper had reached him that the boy was asking for Steve by name. If he knew anything about him then the cripple injured in the helicopter crash should be easy to find. That worried Steve.

It was a problem for a man who liked to know everything but also liked to remain anonymous. Now a face he didn't know was asking for him. He asked one of his most trusted resistance members, Ryan, to find out who the young man was and what he wanted as he carried on wiping down the plastic trays slowly.

He watched as the man he had sent in his place sat down opposite the young man in the clean clothes. A glance to either side by his lieutenant made the other diners give them space in silence. The boy stopped eating and stared at the man opposite him.

"Steve?" he hissed, clearly unsuited to covert operations.

"Who's asking?" said Ryan without looking up from the food he shovelled into his mouth, who was at least five years too young and a head too short to be Steve.

"My name's Max," Max said, feeling sorely obvious in a room full of people wearing rough and stained clothing. Perhaps changing out of his crisp, white shirt first would've been sensible. "And I need to tell you something," he finished urgently.

"Ok, *Max*," said Ryan, finally looking up to see a boy he guessed was genuinely scared, "what do you need to say?"

He leaned down to the table, making it obvious to anyone who was watching that he was trying to impart secrets. "A guard got killed last night," he hissed, louder than it would have sounded if he had just spoken softly. That came as no surprise to Ryan, as the day's feverish activity had all been centred around the murder of a guard in the night. It was common knowledge. When he carried on eating and didn't respond, Max pushed further.

"By another guard," he said.

Ryan stopped chewing.

"Why would a guard kill another guard?" he asked, careful not to say anything that would imply he had anything but a casual interest in what the boy was saying.

"Not here," Max muttered, glancing side to side and further betraying that he was hardly spy material. "Steve, I need—"

"I'm not Steve," Ryan said, resuming his eating as the young man opposite made a face of sheer horror that he had exposed himself. Ryan decided that whilst fear could be faked, this level of desperate incompetence could not.

"But I am interested in your little story. Tell me some more of it so I can sleep tonight."

Max looked horrified. He had no idea what to do next and hadn't even considered not being able to speak to Steve directly. He wasn't fully committed yet, but he had gone too far. If what he had said was reported then he would not live for long. Even if Richards believed him he doubted the brothers would take kindly to any inquiry into the death they had already explained away to further their own cause. Lost for answers as to his next move, Max just sat there as Ryan finished his food.

"Come on," Ryan prompted him. "Hypothetically, why would a guard kill another guard?"

Deciding that he had little else to lose, Max told him.

"Because they want to take over, and the dead man tried to warn me. I mean the Major," he blurted out as quietly as his nerves would allow. He clearly spoke more loudly than he intended as the woman sat to his left shuffled further away as though the mere mention of Richards brought with it an inherent danger. Looking up at Ryan he felt a glimmer of hope that he had finally said something worthy of an audience.

"Who are you?" Ryan asked carefully.

"I'm Max," Max said again, with an equal measure of care, "and I'm Richards's bloody secretary. I heard everything this morning. And there's more—" he said before Ryan cut him off.

"Not here," he said simply. "Finish your food and don't say another word. To anyone, understand me?"

Max nodded, and ate his food as instructed. Ryan calmly got up and walked away to deposit his tray in the spot where they were cleaned. He didn't see the man speak to anyone else, although he was careful not to stare. He finished his food, taking his time, and waited as long as he could before getting up and taking his tray to where the others were stacked. Looking around he saw no sign of Ryan, or indeed of anyone he recognised as he had been plucked out of a work party which didn't stay in the camp much. He handed his tray to the man stacking them with a thank you, but was surprised to find that the tray was pushed back towards him. Looking at the man who had jostled him he heard a whispered question.

"Where do you sleep?" the voice hissed.

Looking incredulously at the stooped man in front of him he thought initially to refuse to answer, but a sudden flash of all the combined intelligence reports he had compiled into a web chart went through his head. The web was synonymous with a spider; the unseen assassin hiding in the shadows. All of the useless pieces of paper, those endless half-overheard conversations and fruitless rumours, all of it was true. And at the heart of the web was Steve.

"Headquarters. Three windows in from the kitchens," he said, hoping that this was the best way to explain it quickly.

"Go," said the man, snatching away the tray. Max went, walking slowly back to his room. Maybe he was cut out for spy work after all.

~

Max lay on his bed well after dark fighting off sleep. He had no way of knowing how he would be contacted, or even if it would be that night. Just as he contemplated changing his clothes and giving in to sleep he sensed a shadow at his window. Stifling the unmanly yell of fright which rose in his chest he opened the clasp and swung the heavy metal frame out, wincing at the small noise it made. Wordlessly and without invitation the shadow placed both hands on the frame and hauled itself into the room making Max scurry back.

The shadow sat on his bed and pulled back his hood, revealing the stooped old man who cleaned the trays in the dining area. Only he wasn't an old man now, he was alert and strong.

"Steve?" Max whispered.

"Yes," Steve answered, "and I'm guessing you know how much danger I'm putting myself in trusting you now, so tell me everything you know."

Max told him. Told him everything.

Steve listened, asked questions to clarify when he needed to, and finally gave Max instructions which ended in a rudimentary method of contacting him.

Climbing back out of the window and slipping through the shadows to his own bed, excitement and fear slugging it out in an even battle in his mind.

⁓

Sleep didn't find Steve that night. He lay dead still on his back, eyes on the dark ceiling as he suffered the mocking sounds of others at slumber. His mind ran through a series of choices, and the way he logically explored them was to imagine a corridor. The corridor had doors either side; some were locked and others weren't. Those he could open often led to other doors and ways to get into the rooms where the access was denied, and he kept retracing his steps – following the reverse course along his trail of breadcrumbs, to keep a mental road map of his route.

All night he explored the dark corridors of his mind, seeing which doors led somewhere and which were best kept firmly shut. As the light began to turn the windows of the room grey instead of black, he got up and stretched his cramped muscles. Dressing in silence he slipped from the room, careful to over-pronounce the limp in case any half-awake eyes watched him, and walked out into the cold morning air.

Wandering slowly to one of his favourite spots near the livestock pens, carefully avoiding the pigs in case they saw him and made the cacophonous noise they did expecting scraps from him, he stood on the dewy grass at a fence and watched.

He watched the sun creep slowly higher, inching above the sky-line. Steve rested his hands on the strand of barbed wire on top of the fence and breathed out heavily. He finally had a plan. His plan had plans, and within those plans other plans needed to work or be standing by to work. The time was rapidly approaching, and it terrified him.

IT MUST BE A TRICK

Lexi had endured the questioning for as long as she felt able to. It may have been weeks, but she feared it was most likely days. The endless cycle of moving rooms and being restrained in different positions; one standing, one sitting on a stool with no possible way to get her back comfortable, and once she was even put it a box which was too short to stand up in but at the same time too narrow to sit.

Each of the rooms differed in their peripheral torture too. Bright lights on in one, loud music in another, inky blackness inside the box.

But then the rooms no longer followed the same pattern and where she expected to be sitting under harsh lights on the same small stool she now found herself with her bound hands tied to a hook in the ceiling forcing her to stand. These factors combined to do exactly what they had been designed to do, and she broke.

She had cried, screamed in rage until her voice cracked, and bawled that she would tell them anything they wanted to know. She repeated this over and over, sagging her body weight until the pain in her hands became unbearable again and then used her legs to support herself until they too became too weary and she repeated the cycle.

The sound of a metal bolt sliding open outside the room made her stop her mumbling and look at the door expectantly. It opened, but only enough to allow an unseen body to place a battered stereo inside the door and it was closed again. The stereo was obviously switched on from outside and the deafening sound of heavy metal music tore through her head and filled the room. Her shouts and pleading were drowned out and she just alternated between standing and dangling until the music came to a stop.

Glancing at the source of her most recent torment, she was struck by the retro and archaic nature of the noise.

"Who uses cassette tapes any more?" she asked out loud, her voice barely more than a whisper.

A tapping sound to her right caught her attention, and she found that the brightly coloured parrot had returned to her. Smiling at it as though she silently thanked it for keeping her company, she asked it the same question in her thoughts that she had just said aloud. The parrot heard her, but in answer it merely cocked its head and visibly shrugged the tops of its folded wings in an approximation of a human shrugging their shoulders.

Well, you're helpful today, she thought, inciting the parrot to squawk in protest at her tone.

Sorry, she thought to it, hoping to appease the insult she had caused.

The bird seemed to accept her apology, and waddled closer to her with its curious gait until it presented itself at her feet and craned its neck up to look her in the eyes.

Turning its head sideways to give her the full and direct attention of one shiny eye, it clicked its tongue and spoke.

"They're going to kill you. It's a trap."

Lexi's world flashed white and the sudden pain in her hands and the stiffness in her lolling neck were unimaginable. The door banged open, two men walked in and threw a bag over her head.

If she had been more alert she would have noticed the irony that whenever this happened in movies, the person wearing the bag would be able to see and hear clues about where they were going and what was happening.

In reality, her breathing was so hard and panicked that she could hear nothing above the rapid, rasping breaths she took and nor could she see anything at all. The only sense seemingly still working was smell, and that was of little use because all she could smell was the musty stench of the sack her head was in.

She did know that she was bundled into a vehicle and driven over bumpy ground before the monotonous song of tyres on smooth tarmac became almost hypnotic. The vehicle stopped and her hands were cut free, still not one word had been spoken to her so she decided it was best to keep the hood on and say nothing. She tried to stay awake and alert, but her body and mind were so utterly exhausted and had been stretched so far beyond tolerable limits that she gave in to the comfortable seat and slept.

She woke in silence.

Breathing and listening for as long as she could, she raised a tentative hand to the hood and pulled it down.

She was alone in the vehicle, the vehicle was alone in picturesque landscape, and her eyes rested on the keys hanging from the ignition.

Slowly she looked around, fearful that whoever was guarding her was watching and waiting for her to make a move so that they had an excuse to kill her.

She saw nobody.

As carefully as she could, she lifted one stiff leg over the central transmission tunnel, followed by the other, as she slid herself over to the driver's seat. The sudden stab of familiarity hit her then, and she realised she was in their Land Rover. Too exhausted, too frightened and half insensible from her treatment, she remembered that there should have been three others with her.

All warnings from her subconscious via the parrot were forgotten, and she started the engine. Not waiting to find out if the engine sparking into life had attracted any attention, she forced her left foot onto the clutch, snatched a gear with her left hand, and planted the throttle to drive away.

Dropping the binoculars to hang on the cord around his neck, Leo turned to Sabine and smiled.

It was not a warm smile, she doubted he was capable of genuine emotions, but she gathered that he intended it to be.

"Bite, little fishes," he growled.

STAND READY

Inside Sanctuary was a buzz of activity. Of the contingent originally from their inland farm who had migrated to the coast in order to bolster the fishing strength over the winter, a dozen were chosen to be issued with, and trained in the basic use of, some brand new assault rifles.

The previously peaceful pacifists took the news well with no exceptions, willing volunteers all, and although none felt as though they would find themselves in peril they were happy enough to fire an entire magazine over the sea in single shots under tuition from Mitch, Leah and Dan before being given two full magazines and sent home. They would soon have to resume the planting cycle of vegetables and other crops, just as they had done the previous year.

Dan marvelled at this and wondered if he hadn't taken charge of their old group back home, if the others still there would have formed such a well-structured cooperative system without instruction. Shaking that away as an irrelevance, he watched as the relatively large group walked up the approach road inland to head to their homes and loved ones. Soon, the flow of supplies would begin to reverse and they would see new harvests of fruit, vegetables and other stuff he didn't know how to grow coming to the impenetrable fortress.

The town's defences were set, and he had even allowed test firing of both heavy machine guns. They worked, and that was all he needed to know. They could hardly afford to expend the rare ammunition unless they were forced to defend themselves. The anti-tank rockets were a matter for much discussion, and it had been agreed that they would only be used in dire emergencies by people who knew what they were doing. Which, if he really thought about it, was absolutely nobody; they were all pretty much making this up on the spot.

Polly was in the process of forming a guard rota, but seeing as most of the firearms-capable residents were from Dan's group she was trying to organise more from the town's population to volunteer.

Deciding that it was time, he eventually made the back-breaking climb to the fort and resupply the defenders who spent much of their time in the clouds, given the poor weather at that time of year. Briefly discussing the best way to carry the arms and ammunition up the intensely steep stone staircase, it was quickly decided that Neil would wait at the foot of the cliffs on the approach road and attach a bundle to the rope they planned to drop from the parapets when they arrived.

Stripping down to his t-shirt and equipment vest and making sure they all carried a bottle of water, Dan set off with Ash behind him. Leah and Mitch followed, along with a couple others rostered to swap with the existing defenders and allow for some time off. One of these was carrying a large backpack of personal items, and since he had asked to be sent to the fort to save his embarrassment, Dan had seen or heard nothing of Olivier.

Standing at the bottom and looking up, the dark shaft revealed only a pinprick of light at the top. He knew that the pinprick was in fact a full-sized door, and the impossibly small size of it betrayed just how far away they were. Adjusting the grip on his new rifle in his left hand, he shifted the weight of the long coil of rope over his right shoulder.

Head down, arse up, he heard barked from the furthest recesses of his memory, back to when he struggled as a teenaged recruit on long forced marches.

He smiled at the renewed meaning of that saying, repeated it to himself and thinking each word in turn with every footfall on a new step.

Head.

Down.

Arse.

Up.

Within a few minutes, despite setting an intentionally steady pace, his skin prickled with sweat and his breathing had become rapid. There was a reason, he thought sourly, why people in the gym always looked so exhausted after using the stair machines.

Calling a halt at what he felt must be the quarter way mark, he sat on a step and handed the heavy coil of rope to Mitch who was due to carry it next. Taking long pulls from the tube on the shoulder of his vest and working to empty the small water bladder built into it, he poured some water from his bottle into his palm and let Ash coat his outstretched hand with hot, greasy drool. Wiping his hand on the dog's coat he was rewarded with a sticky hand now covered in loose fur, and not a dry hand as he intended. Sighing to himself he wiped the hand on the leg of his fading black trousers. The shiny swathe it left dried his hand, but successfully left the residue making his hand feel sticky. Ash seemed unconcerned about spoiling Dan's laundry schedule, and instead looked at him for more. Deciding that he'd already got covered in dribble, he had little else to lose. Pouring Ash another handful of water, the dog tickled his palm as the massive tongue shot out to retrieve the precious liquid.

Climbing to his feet and feeling the dizzying sensation of gravity pulling him inexorably back to sea level, he wobbled slightly. Glancing back up the staircase with a steadying hand on the rough stone wall, he felt that he may have underestimated the distance covered.

Repeating his new mantra over and over in his head, he led the group upwards until, many minutes and three more stops later, they emerged wheezing and sweating into the cold sunlight.

They were in the sky, and the view was unparalleled to anything he had ever seen before in his life.

"That is why... they don't walk... to work every day," Mitch said between big lungfuls of air before drinking from a bottle and draining it. Although fit enough and certainly fitter than the average person, Dan, Mitch and Leah were in need of a quiet place to sit down for five minutes before being able to think clearly or speak. It was not only the leg-cramping, lung-bursting climb but the rapid increase in altitude which combined to temporarily ruin them.

A bowl of water was brought for Ash by a young Frenchman, little more than a boy really, who regarded the big dog with fond eyes. Ash, capricious as ever, returned the admiration as the boy had brought him something.

As an instant character judge the dog's instincts were unmatched, unless someone brought him food then that judgement became clouded.

Greeting the defenders, which were – to Dan's mind – too few to make any real defensive difference, he toured the ramparts which were in good repair and obviously kept clean and clear. There was an assortment of weapons on display, none of which were much use apart from one impressive hunting rifle with a large optic. The owner of that gun sported a huge moustache and spoke no English, but through a translator Dan learned a little about him and he felt reassured that the owner was as capable as his gun.

The long rope was linked to two others by sturdy knots and cast hard over the wall where it sailed through the air and fell to whiplash against the stone cliff face below. Neil's frantic and exaggerated waving, as reported through a watcher using a rifle scope, meant that more rope had to be found as it was not long enough. A brief pause until a long length of chain was found gave time for awkward silences, but eventually their tether was fixed to a large bundle containing the ten new rifles destined for use in the fort.

The defenders were assembled and taught the basics of how to handle, fire, reload and clear the weapon in the highly unlikely event of a jam, whilst below the first of three more bundles containing ammunition and other supplies were being hauled skywards.

Dan, Leah and Mitch spent the remainder of the morning working with them to ensure they were comfortable with the guns. Neil's final package included the small radio set complete with battery pack and the car alternator charging system they had pioneered in postapocalyptic France. This allowed two-way communication with the gatehouse, where similar sets were proudly in place to speak to the sea-facing gun battery, the watchtower and now the fort.

As the last package inched its way up the cliff face, someone spoke in urgent French and grabbed Dan's attention. He did not understand the words, but he understood the tone.

Trouble.

Running over to the fire step and leaning out to look down, despite his feelings of discomfort with heights, Dan raised his weapon to use the telescopic sight. Seeing Neil retreating at speed towards the

155

gate was the first activity his scope found, and he panned the barrel to his right to find the cause of the sudden panic.

The moustached man said a single word which Dan did understand, even though he saw it as soon as his brain translated what he heard.

"Voiture."

There was indeed a car. It was instantly familiar, yet so out of place that it couldn't possibly be there. No matter how hard Dan looked at it as he followed its progress through the optic, he could not deny that it was really there. He even recognised the custom modifications Neil had made to it by adding an extra fuel tank to the roof.

"That's impossible," he said aloud as he was flanked by Leah who also took aim with her own gun to see the approaching vehicle.

Leah gasped but said nothing. She knew why Dan was so incredulous.

The last time they saw that Land Rover, they were sailing away from the south coast of England.

"Simon?" Mitch said incredulously from Dan's left, where he too used his new rifle's scope to magnify the image. "What the fuck is he doing here?"

Nobody had an answer, but all three made for the stairs to find out.

It came to Dan's mind that anyone who believed going down stairs was easier than going up them, was an idiot. They were an idiot who had never even dreamt of a staircase as big as this, either.

Not only did each downward step cause their already burning leg muscles to ache more, the fear of losing his footing made the experience infinitely more stressful; tripping down those stairs would almost certainly result in a mild case of death.

He reached the bottom ahead of the others and jumped the last few steps to land with both feet. Hitting the deck heavily and biting his tongue in the process, he realised that his dead legs were not going to forgive him for that stupidity as both had collapsed on impact.

Forcing himself unsteadily upright he heard a question shouted from behind, but had no breath to answer that he was fine and merely waved an exhausted hand to signify that he wasn't damaged.

Deciding against any more attempts to run, he hobbled as fast as he could manage towards the gatehouse.

From behind the heavy wooden doors he could hear the unmistakable tone of the diesel engine, and unthinkingly threw the heavy locking bar out of position to open the gateway.

"WAIT!" bawled a voice from behind him, making him pause briefly and reassess. His brain could conjure no conceivable reason for their old vehicle to be there, nor how it crossed the channel, or how it had found them despite the thousands of miles they had covered in between.

Deciding that he needed answers to these questions more than he needed to wait, he threw open the door and froze.

Twenty feet away, sat stock still behind the wheel, were the wide eyes and greasy blonde hair of Lexi.

UNTOLD DAMAGE

Later, much later, Dan's mind wandered to consider just how autonomous driving was. Like riding a bike. Even when someone was catatonic, dehydrated, and completely absent from the world they could still operate the controls as though they were extensions of themselves. That thought seemed almost irrelevant, like a self-imposed distraction designed to protect the mind from the horrors it had witnessed.

It had taken him near on thirty seconds to come to terms that he was actually facing the young woman he had left in England so many months ago. She was, undeniably, right there in front of him, but he had no idea how any of the necessary factors to make it possible for her to be here had come to pass. She sat behind the wheel, eyes wide and knuckles white as her bony hands gripped the worn leather. The engine idled until the foot holding down the clutch gave way and the car jolted forward to stall and rolled until her instincts cut in again and her right foot stabbed onto the brake. Dan had leapt aside, and pulled open the driver's door.

The girl inside didn't respond or even turn to look at him as he reached over her to pull on the handbrake.

The first thing to hit him was the smell. She clearly hadn't washed in a long time, but it was more her actions – or lack of actions – which really disturbed him.

"Lex," he said, half as a question and half as a statement of disbelief. She didn't respond.

"*Lexi*," he said more intensely, shaking her right arm gently.

Her breathing changed, like she had awoken or was startled, and she switched her gaze down to meet Dan's eyes.

He gasped involuntarily. If the eyes are a window to the soul, then he stared through the window into emptiness. He saw glassy, bloodshot orbs devoid of all life shining back at him. Shaking her arm again he repeated her name with intensity as though he could will her to return to the present. For a flash she was back, the glassiness in her eyes turning instantly to tears as the floodgates opened.

Collapsing into hysterical sobs she fell from the cab and into his arms. He held her weight easily, feeling her bones through her filthy clothes, and hefted her up to carry her like a child. Negotiating the gap in the heavy gates he bawled for Kate.

Leah, sweating and red-faced from her rapid descent from the fort, stared wide-eyed for a second until she gathered her wits and decided that questions could wait. Turning on her heel she sprinted away to fetch and prepare their paramedic to receive the incoming patient.

Bundling into the main hall and prompting startled looks from the few people present, she scanned the room and saw that Kate was not there. Turning again she ran towards the rooms designated as the medical centre for their community and saw Kate coming from the room. Opening her mouth to ask what was happening, instantly gathering that there was a problem, Leah spoke first and cut her off.

"Lexi's here. Alone. Dan's bringing her up, unconscious," she said, succinct and breathless.

Kate said nothing, other than to mouth, *what the fuck?* in silent response to the unexpected information. Turning back into the room she selected a cleared space and began to grab the necessary equipment to monitor a patient's vitals with deft and experienced hands.

Seconds later the door burst open and Dan entered carrying the limp form of the girl nobody expected to see again. Kate's eyes stung from the acidic aura emanating from her but her professionalism pushed that unwelcome discomfort aside.

"What happened to her?" she asked the room in general.

"Don't know," Dan said, breathing hard. "She pulled up at the gates and was catatonic then she passed out." He was about to tell Kate to check her eyes but she was ahead of him, shining a tiny torch into them and tutting instinctively at how bloodshot they were.

Working fast and smoothly she checked the young woman over and settled back to regard her sleeping form critically.

"She's exhausted. Literally," she announced. "Malnourished, dehydrated. The only time I'd see someone like this is when they've been trapped somewhere," she finished as she was inserting a needle in Lexi's bare arm to flush her body with fluids.

"Or held captive," Dan said ominously, glancing at Leah. Unbidden, she nodded and turned away heading for the gate to renew the guard.

She issued orders and watched them until they moved with a purpose, albeit an uncomprehending one. Snatching up the radio sets to the tower and the fort in turn she brought their eyes in the sky up to speed and finished with an instruction to stay alert.

Deciding to clear the obstruction in front of their gates she ordered the archway opened and drove the truck carefully through the narrow gateway and into the tight, cobbled streets inside.

The smell inside the cab was bad, forcing Leah to lean out of the window for fresh air. Parking it near to the small docks away from the gatehouse, she killed the engine and glanced around the cab. Something was off, other than the smell.

There was no equipment, no bags, nothing in the car. For people who habitually carried their 'go' bags everywhere they went containing the necessary survival equipment should disaster strike, that was just plain weird.

Climbing down from the cab she walked to the rear door and pulled it open, finding a blanket covering a large lump. Whipping it away, she found the source of the smell wasn't just Lexi.

Under the blanket, swollen faced and horribly bruised, lay an unconscious Paul.

~

All eyes, despite the warnings from Leah, were focussed inside the walls after the commotion she raised on finding Paul. From high on the cliffs looking down onto the fort and the walled town below stood four figures, each looking through binoculars or weapon mounted optics.

"Let's see how your *rot* takes now, Sabine," said the expressionless man in his gruff voice.

"Let them worry for now," she answered, "then we send them another gift."

None of the others answered, merely turned away to return to the second phase of their plan.

It was ten days before Christmas, and they believed that the New Year would bring them victory.

WHISKEY, TANGO, FOXTROT

Dan could not begin to comprehend what events had transpired to present Lexi to the gates, and the discovery of Paul evidently beaten to within an inch of his life only added to his confusion.

He desperately wanted answers, but neither one of them were in a position to provide them; Lexi remained unconscious despite physically being relatively unharmed, and even when Paul regained consciousness he could not speak.

Kate had far greater concern for him than he did Lexi. She said that the girl's body had simply shut down to protect itself and repair, whereas Paul was in immediate need of medical care.

She listed his injuries, those that she could diagnose without x-rays, and it made for grim reading.

"Severely concussed, jaw fractured on the left side and probably an orbital break too," she reeled off. Dan had broken his eye socket once years ago and remembered with a grimace how long it took him to recover.

"His hands are broken too, judging by the boot prints in the bruising I'd say they were stamped on," she said, continuing the damage report. "Ribs too, and other than that I can't tell until the swelling goes down. He's pissing blood, too, which could be a whole raft of things which may or may not be life-threatening. For now, all we can do is give him pain killers and anti-inflammatory meds and hope for the best."

Her normal rising anger at seeing people hurt was oddly absent, given the sheer destructive level of the beating Paul had taken. She seemed more pale than normal.

Dan opened his mouth to speak but she cut him off quietly.

"I don't know when they will be awake, and even then I don't know if they'll be able to tell you much."

Dan closed his mouth. Placing a hand on her shoulder he left the room and went to Marie as he had been instructed to. She was probably within seven weeks of giving birth now, and the medication left her frail and drawn. Still, she smiled when he walked in and rested his rifle against the wall. Melting heavily into a chair, Dan loosened his boots without taking them off as Ash mirrored his exhausted flop by hitting the rug in front of an open coal fire.

"Kate has no idea when they'll wake up," he said, noisily undoing the Velcro of his vest in some small concession to comfort.

"Paul is badly hurt and physically can't speak, Lexi is in some kind of emotional coma by the look of it." He sighed, rubbed his face as though he could force out the confusion and infuse some answers.

"They're alive and they're here. Everything else we'll figure out," Marie told him, as anxious as she felt she knew it didn't pay to wind him up any further when he felt powerless.

The litany of questions had come in a salvo of such ferocity that anyone listening would have thought Dan was angry. He was, but he just had that unfortunate manner that the person he was speaking to seemed to take the brunt of everything.

"Anyway, how are you feeling?" he said, changing the subject to something he hoped was far happier.

"Fine," she said. "Don't worry about me. Kate says I'm doing well and nothing is wrong; the baby's heartbeat is strong." Glancing at Dan she saw his eyes had closed and his head leaned back in the chair. She carried on talking, unsure if he was listening much but feeling no annoyance as her man hadn't stopped for long or even slept much in the last five days. Testing her theory, she trailed off to see if he noticed.

Eyes still closed and mouth still slightly open, Dan surprised her by still being awake.

"Need to decide on a name," he said groggily. "What was your father called?"

"We're not naming her after my father," she said with a smile, returning to one of their usual sources for friendly disagreement.

"He'll need a good, strong name," Dan said, still checking the back of his eyelids.

"Yes," Marie said, "*she* will."

Dan smiled, before he went the way of his dog and fell asleep where he sat.

~

Dan woke, neck in stiff agony, to find the fire burned down and Marie still asleep in bed a few feet away. Glancing down to his right he saw what had woken him as Ash licked his right hand again and regarded him expectantly.

The dog's stomach was more accurate than any timepiece he had ever worn.

Leaning over to feel the warm breath coming from Marie he quietly left after picking up his rifle and shutting the door as silently as possible.

Stopping on the stone steps to tie his boots, he told Ash he would have to wait as they went via medical to get food.

Entering the makeshift hospital, all thoughts of food were forgotten.

Lexi was sat up, awake.

She had clearly been treated to a shower, evidently her first for a long time, and her long, wet hair had changed colour from when he saw her last. Her eyes held far more presence than when he had last seen them, but she still wore an air of vacancy that was unnatural on her.

Dan walked over and started to bombard her with questions as softly as he could, but when she recoiled in child-like fear he stopped. Kate rose and gently pulled him away by the elbow. The paramedic looked exhausted too, evidently having spent the night watching over them both. Sera joined them from the next room where Paul was suffering silently. She too looked tired.

"She hasn't spoken yet," Kate said in a low warning, "and I'm not sure she will yet. Someone really fucked these two up."

Dan already had his suspicions given his own fairly recent treatment at the hands of others, but he decided not to start a chorus of jungle drums just yet and cause panic.

"She's acting like a mute child," Kate continued, "which must be some sort of defence mechanism."

Dan turned to regard his former Ranger and saw only the frightened child Kate had alluded to. So many thoughts bounced around his head which could only be forced into any semblance of order by answers; answers that Paul was too damaged to give and Lexi was too frightened to.

Wearing a warm, fatherly smile Dan pulled up the chair next to Lexi's bed.

"Do you remember me?" he asked her softly.

Lexi's eyes flickered between Dan's face and Ash. She nodded, but kept her lips forcefully pursed.

"You're safe here. We call this place Sanctuary," he said.

At the mention of the name, Lexi's eyes grew wide and she fired glances around the room as though searching desperately for safety. Pure terror in her eyes, she stared at him as though caught out and in trouble as her breathing became rapid and her still bloodshot eyes welled up with tears. Her head shook from side to side in disbelief until she finally spoke.

"What is Sanctuary?" she asked, her voice full of malice and anger as though not her own.

"Where are you from?" she said, rising from the bed with a furious look on her face.

"What are you DOING HERE?" she screamed.

Dan's look of confusion seemed to enrage her and she screamed again, baring her teeth and lashing out at him. He leapt back as he got to his feet, Ash stepping forward and issuing a frightened bark at what was happening.

"What is Sanctuary?" she screamed, repeating the question hysterically before bursting out in tears and hiding under the blankets of her bed where she sobbed forcefully, leaving the three shocked people and one confused dog staring at her.

"I want to wake up!" she sobbed. "Just let me wake up."

"You *are* awake," Sera told her, reaching out a tentative hand to touch her shoulder and making her recoil, "and you're safe here," she added.

"*Safe?*" she snapped savagely. "Fucking *safe?*" whipping back the covers from her head she regarded them through teary eyes suddenly more angry than upset with her wet hair plastered to her face.

"Nowhere is safe," she spat, "he'll find you."

In that moment, Dan knew with absolute certainty who had delivered his two broken friends back to him, but he still had to ask.

"*HIM!*" Lexi answered. "He made Steve crash. He took everyone. Simon. Chris," she ranted, confusing everyone.

Seeing his own confusion mirrored in Kate and Sera, he turned back to Lexi to see she had regressed to the scared, childlike state she had been in before.

"They're all gone," she cried, "the Frenchman told me."

Even more confused, Dan was lost for words. He had no way to know that Lexi was so confused, her mind a broken jigsaw puzzle of facts that could not fit together yet. He knew enough, however, to be fairly sure of two things: one, they were not safe there, not yet, and two, that all was not well at their old home.

THE MIXING POT

Steve's recently acquired intelligence source was a goldmine. Max provided locations of weapons storage, provided numbers and rotation times of guards, and even more information kept secret from the general population.

The camp had somehow established contact with survivors in other countries – Canada and Spain that Max knew of – although they were obviously as cagey with details as anyone would be given the circumstances. Max didn't know how this contact had been made, and didn't know the location of what was called the 'communications room' on the reports crossing his desk.

He knew that others had found a way around *the baby problem*, as Richards called it, but knew little else about it.

He also kept tabs as best he could on the activity of the two brothers, although they kept their own dedicated guard units insulated from the rest of the command structure and gave their own orders in interpretation of those Richards cascaded out via Max.

Steve thought of ways he could use Max's influential position to undermine the leadership, but everything he came up with posed a risk to the young man. He couldn't accept that, at least not yet. That gave him pause; was he really capable of putting someone in danger for his greater good?

Had Steve become that person?

The answer took little soul-searching, and it was yes.

Yes, he would put Max at risk, as he would himself or anyone else, but only when the results outweighed the cost of losing the resource.

He hadn't done this, he told himself: they had. They had taken him and his friends away from their home, had hurt and killed people, had removed their liberty and provided a dubious safety at the cost of their liberty.

He had become the man who was prepared to do what it took to remove Richards, only now the scenario was complicated by the brothers – or the twins as his people still called them – who were vying for control themselves.

Rubbing his eyes as he lay awake in bed he tried to clear his mind in the hope that sleep wouldn't elude him again that night. He knew he was kidding himself; sleep would not come while his mind burned off a thousand different possibilities.

⁓

"I say we move with what we have in place already," Will said vehemently, looking into his brother's eyes which betrayed nothing.

Benjamin said nothing. Merely stared back for a few heartbeats until Will's momentum expended itself in the silence.

"Don't rush it," he said simply, "last time you rushed things you brought in a man we – I – had to kill to keep us all alive."

Will said nothing, the stress of their near miss of discovery still causing him sleepless nights. They had got away with it though, only just, and their secret was still safe amongst the few they trusted. They decided not to expand the inner circle any further, believing that most guards and other people involved in the organisation would simply accept the change in leadership as it would make little difference to their everyday lives.

"We stick to the plan," Benjamin repeated patiently, "and take over on New Year's Eve when we get Richards drunk and make it look like an accident. Then I announce that I'm taking over as second in command; people like the natural order. That way we won't look like traitors and things just carry on as normal," he finished, repeating each step as though talking to an impatient child.

They had discussed many ways to remove Richards from the equation. A couple of key others would need to go quietly too, but that could be done in slow time. They could be called outside of the camp on urgent business and never return, that part would be simple enough. Killing Richards outright would cause a commotion, and with emotions running high, who knows what could happen in the heat of the moment. They planned a bloodless, well almost bloodless, coup and on New Year's Eve when people were permitted to celebrate then Richards would drink too much and die in a fall. A tragic accident. An event of public mourning, no matter how insincere, would follow and then Will's leadership would be accepted without challenge.

If there were to be any challenge, then they agreed that further accidents were always possible.

ROCKS AND HARD PLACES

Dan was stuck. Frustrated.

When he was frustrated, he recognised, he was a bit of an arse to be around. He found himself snapping at people he would ordinarily have asked kindly to help him. He yelled at his dog for being under his feet, when Ash was only there out of an utterly undying and unquestioning loyalty.

Dan's insight into his behaviour only served to make him feel guilty, which added to his frustration.

He had a horribly ominous feeling about many things. He was certain that the men who had captured him had tortured Lexi and Paul, and that they would eventually have to deal with them once and for all. That held a number of inherent problems: how would they safely get outside of the walls to scavenge further afield? How could they protect the farms, their power supply and the few people maintaining the wind turbine? Taking enough fighters out of the protection afforded by the walls meant leaving amateurs manning complex and dangerous machinery, and his suspicious nature didn't really want to be outside of the gate in the killing field of such a massive machine gun when he didn't fully trust the person controlling it. All of these concerns were overshadowed by the feeling of dread when he recalled the man whose nose he had broken and feared that this may all be his doing, like it was personal.

And those were just the immediate problems.

He also worried constantly about Marie who seemed to be getting both bigger and weaker by the day, and there was still the risk to the baby and her from childbirth.

He worried about what sequence of events could possibly have come to pass that led Lexi and Paul to be thousands of miles away from home with no equipment. He worried about the things Lexi had said, her insane rantings which had caused Kate to have to sedate her as he held her down onto the hospital bed.

He also now, just to add another item to his list of shit stopping him sleeping, had to worry about another pregnancy. The morning after Lexi's arrival saw another visit to the gate, this time two people from the farm with a dog in tow.

They had no idea, how could they, about the events the previous day. Being told that they had to stay in Sanctuary for their own safety came as a disappointing blow, but the couple understood. They had brought their dog as it needed veterinary care, and Ash, it seemed, was the cause.

The cross-breed bitch he had met during the resupply run with Mitch and Leah was now, undeniably, pregnant. Sera made loud noises about having enough to do already, but Dan knew the frosty woman well enough to know that her bluster covered the fact that she warmed to the dog immediately and would enjoy a brief return to her old life and see these puppies into the world with joy. She examined the bitch as thoroughly as she could and gave a rough estimate as to when the litter was due.

Around the time Marie was due to give birth.

So, on top of all the immediate, long-term and long-distance problems Dan had to worry about, Neil made it worse by happily reminding him that he will soon be a father and a technical grandfather all around the same time.

Seeing the silent glance Dan shot towards him prompted a burst of laughter and Neil beat a hasty retreat.

Dan was certain that if he could find out what had happened from Lexi, just the basics of why she had left home and who hurt them, then he could formulate a better plan of what to do. Fighting off the frustration with repeated runs up and down the stone steps didn't work as he became fatigued too fast due to the long days of worrying and watching. Wandering the big castle with so many empty rooms he came across Mitch who was wearing a look he could only describe as guilty.

"What's that for?" Dan asked casually, pointing at the long loop of copper wire slung over his shoulder.

Not one for dishonesty, Mitch answered him.

"Command wire," he said simply, swallowing and keeping his face neutral as though talking to a senior officer in his old life. It was all he could do not to stand to attention.

"Command wire as in for a detonation?" Dan asked carefully, knowing that Mitch retreated behind short answers to protect himself.

"Er, yeah," he replied.

"Two things," Dan said in a measured tone. "Who else knows what you're up to and show me."

He suspected the copper wire would have come from Neil, which it had, and in answer to the command to show Dan what he was planning, Mitch simply walked on and beckoned him to follow.

Walking into an empty room, bare apart from an old wooden table and stool, Dan paused in horror.

"It's safe!" Mitch explained having seen the look on his face. "See, not connected yet!" he finished, waving what looked like short, metal pens connected to more wire at Dan.

The sight of the detonators in Mitch's hand wasn't what was causing Dan concern, but more the two green slabs of metal with their cases prised open did that.

"Vehicle mines," Mitch said, as though explaining what they were would make it any better.

Dan was no munitions expert, at all, but he had a healthy fear and respect for such things that prompted a great deal of worry at seeing abandoned explosives being messed with in such an amateur way. Still backing towards the door, as though a few feet of stone could possibly prevent his atomisation should they inadvertently go off, he kept his eyes on the mess on the table.

"They're completely safe," Mitch said, sitting down on the stool with a seemingly cavalier lack of regard for his own life.

"I need to run enough wire to detonate them on command instead of having something roll over them and get launched," he explained. Dan, still too horrified to answer, just stared at him so he took it as permission to carry on with the explanation.

"You see, normally, you'd bury these buggers under the surface and whatever goes over it cops for the shaped charge firing straight up," he explained with useful sign language indicating a vehicle being launched skywards "but we don't want our vehicles or any friendlies getting blown up. I want to rig these two at the choke point on the road between the cliffs. I'll put them vertically, facing towards each other, and pack rocks over them to make the approach even tighter, like one vehicle width." He paused, waiting for any questions that might have arisen. Seeing Dan still staring, he continued.

"Anyway, long command wire from both to the gun position above the gate, detonator in each, and whack the ends onto a battery. Boom. One attack seriously fucked up." He finished with a beaming smile and two raised thumbs.

Dan still stared at him, half in terror of the destructive power and half in absolute admiration.

"Genius," he said, half in caustic jest and yet grateful for Mitch's untasked activity. Still slightly in shock, he walked away a little faster than normal as he pictured the mess of wires and explosives.

That evening, before the light failed, he helped Mitch, Neil and a handful of volunteers as they moved rocks and piled them back over the mines carefully after they were wrapped in thick, black plastic. Dan stood watch, weapon ready, whilst Leah held the high ground with her battle rifle from the wall above the gate.

The long, copper wire, reclaimed from so many telegraph poles and recycled to become part of a weapon, was laid into a trench scraped through the rocky ground and fed up the wall to where it was fixed in place under the wooden gun shelter where the battery required to fire it was kept dry well away from the wires.

If it worked, and there were many variables which would say it might not work, it would easily devastate anything short of a battle tank coming through that gap.

It was Christmas Eve, and Dan guessed that counted as wrapping a present of sorts.

IMPROVISATION

Mitch wasn't the only person to be reclaiming parts of innocuous machinery with the intention of weaponising it. Working under a bright bulb which occasionally flickered due to the inconsistent power created by an ageing diesel generator, another grizzled man – another soldier – worked with an array of small tools and wires.

Using thick glasses to magnify his work, he used a soldering iron to connect a wire to a ball. The ball had previously been the gear lever for a car, and the man smirked to himself as he imagined what the manufacturers would think now he was using their engineering for destruction.

He connected the loose end of the wire to a small circuit board and depressed the trigger switch which used to be for selecting park, reverse, neutral or drive. Each time he released the switch the small lightbulb on the board lit up faintly.

Satisfied, he picked up another reclaimed part of the same vehicle, this time the air conditioning button. Connecting it similarly, he tested it on the circuit board again and was rewarded with the dim light when he clicked the switch on. He pressed it again and the light went out.

So engrossed was he in his work that he did not notice the man stood leaning languidly in the doorway.

"Damn you, Leo," he grumbled in French, barely able to disguise his small start. "Must you sneak up on everyone?" he complained.

"It is a skill," Leo declared flatly in humourless response. "Is it working?"

"Yes," answered the man. "I assume you have the parts I need?"

In reply, Leo held aloft a small, green canvas bag he had hidden behind his back. Placing it on the desk before him he turned and left.

"I will prepare the delivery method," he said ambiguously from the doorway.

Ignoring the parts of the plan which didn't directly involve him, the man returned to his work and regarded the bag. It was a satchel in drab military colours, and inside were three shapes not too dissimilar to house bricks.

The man knew that inside each brick was a shaped charge of high explosive. He knew the destructive power of a single charge having used them to great effect collapsing metal bridges and creating openings in walls without having to knock on the door. Each charge would explode, if executed correctly, with a directed blast capable of some serious carnage. Three, in the design and configuration he had been asked to create, would flip a small tank.

He had no qualms about what he was asked to do; it simply did not concern him. He was a soldier, he had orders, and he intended to follow them.

Carefully removing the detonators from each charge and separating them, his deft fingers worked fast to check a dry run of how it would work.

Activating the circuit by connecting the air conditioning button via its wire to three 9 volt batteries taped together he clicked the button in.

Holding down the switch of the gear lever in his right hand as he connected that wire to the batteries, he connected the command wire to the bulb on his circuit board. The bulb, in his dry run representing the power to the detonators flashed on as soon as he released the gear lever switch.

"Boom," he said to himself quietly, no trace of humour in his voice.

Removing the wires now that he knew the connections were good, he began stitching the satchel onto a carrying harness.

Leo was satisfied with the attrition rate. One of the men he had captured was aggressive from the start, and had proven himself to be capable. That man had to be beaten so badly that he could not pose a threat. The woman's wits abandoned her quite quickly and there was no point in using violence against her, even though one of his men seemed to take pleasure in hitting her. He had dealt with that man privately and quietly, not out of any sense of propriety but for the fact that he despised emotional responses in soldiers; to feed one's obsession or fetish is to lose sight of the mission goal.

These two he had sent to his quarry with the intent to unsettle him. True, others had argued that this gave the people tucked safely behind the high stone walls time to prepare for an attack, but they didn't know the entire plan. They didn't know about his back door.

In sending the two broken people to him, he had sent a message. He had invoked fear and anger, and frightened and angry people did foolish things under pressure. It was the prelude to looking in the man's eyes as he killed him.

Now, returning his attention to the remaining two captives, he set in motion the final part of the plan to damage the defenders from the inside.

Walking into a room as the guard posted outside nodded to him – seemingly what passed for military discipline now, not that he minded as actions and loyalty were always valued over salutes – Leo sat down calmly on the bed next to the man.

"What are you thinking about?" he asked softly, in a barely audible whisper.

"Dan," came the weak response after a heartbeat.

"You're thinking what he did to you? Why he abandoned you to this fate?" he pressed, his translation adding eloquence to his words.

"Yes," came the answer. "I hate him. It's all his fault."

Making soothing noises he patted the knee of the man who was curled up on a thin mattress like a traumatised child.

"I know," he said, "I know. Soon you will get your chance to avenge everyone he killed."

For the first time the man's eyes raised from where they stared blankly at the bed.

"Really?" he asked.

"Yes, Chris," answered Leo. "I know I can trust you," he said, rising slowly to leave the room.

SO MANY QUESTIONS

Christmas morning came without the fuss of previous years – before or after – and Dan smoked as he stood guard over the gate.

He had been on watch for a little over an hour before a hollering noise penetrated the windswept walkways and reached his ears. It was, although unclear, unmistakably a call for him. He just knew.

Turning to the inky black archway which led to the spiralling stone step down, he saw Mitch emerge red-faced.

"Infirmary," he said, trying to catch his breath. "I'll take over here."

Without a word, Dan strode past him to take the steps as fast as safety allowed. Ash fell behind on the uneven staircase, but easily caught up with him on the straight as he jogged along the corridors.

Bursting into the room he saw everyone flinch. Everyone included Marie, who was sat at the side of Lexi's bed holding her hand.

She was awake, and she seemed to some extent in possession of her faculties.

Nodding with her eyes, Marie indicated that he should wait at the back of the room and listen. Wordlessly he went and kept his eyes down as though that could minimise his presence, but Ash whined and danced on the spot.

Lexi responded to his noise, and held out a hand which he shot forward to nuzzle. Placing one giant paw at a time on the bed he tried to haul himself onto her lap with as much success as trying to play golf with a basketball – he just didn't fit. He did respond to Marie telling him to get down, although made sure he remained in physical contact with Lexi, like he knew she was hurt.

"Ash," Lexi croaked with a smile, looking to Marie to check if her memory was correct and not distorted.

"Yes," Marie replied. "You remember Ash."

Lexi smiled wider and stroked the big dog's head.

"Lexi," Marie said carefully, "tell me again what happened."

Lexi's eyes remained resolutely unfocussed in the direction of the dog as her words began to flow.

"Steve crashed coming back. Bad," she said in a small voice. "The twins took over and an army came for us. We escaped and came to find you. Simon found us. The Frenchman caught us."

The room remained in total silence disturbed only by Ash yawning. All eyes apart from Lexi's panned to him, as though he could make sense of her answer.

It had taken Marie over an hour to reassure Lexi and get her to speak. The broken girl had more questions than answers at first, and it was clear she didn't trust her own memory of events. Marie would say so, but she had reservations about the accuracy of Lexi's recollection too; it was clear the girl had become detached from reality at some point and was struggling to reintegrate.

Filing outside of the door quietly and leaving Ash comforting Lexi, they formed a small circle in the corridor and spoke in hushed voices.

"So, Steve is badly hurt in a helicopter crash we're assuming?" Dan began. "Twins took over the prison and an army took everyone away, somehow Simon came with them and they were captured." He recapped, seeing no disagreement but a worrying amount of discomfort on the other faces around him.

"It's got to be that bastard who captured me," he said, finally voicing what he had been thinking for a few days. "And his only reason for sending them back to us is to screw with our heads or they work for him. I think it's the former," he announced, again meeting no disagreement.

"So what do we do?" asked Marie, seemingly on behalf of everyone.

"We wait for him to come, then we kill him," Dan said, seeing mouths open in preparation to protest. "We don't have the strength to take it to him and leave this place defended," he said, cutting them off before they started. "So what other choice do we have?"

Silence.

"We could try to talk to them?" offered Kate, ever hopeful for an outcome which didn't involve the risk of injury or death for anyone, but her head dropped and she answered her own thoughts aloud. "But seeing what they've done to Lex and Paul I doubt they're much into talking," she finished. Silence again.

"So we end them. We fucking kill them all," came a quiet voice. Everyone turned to face Polly; the peace-loving, naïve and trusting woman who was the last person anyone would have suspected would suggest violence.

Maybe that was because she hadn't seen any yet.

"Am I the only one who is terrified of these people?" she said in alarm at the faces regarding her.

"No," said a voice coming from down the corridor, having heard the discussion as she approached silently. "You're not. It's just that I said something similar last time we were attacked and they all looked at me like I was insane too."

Without offering any further input, Leah walked straight past the group and into the room where it was obvious from the sounds coming through the open door that Lexi recognized her.

Returning to his spot above the gatehouse Dan lit a cigarette and inhaled deeply, letting the smoke dissipate instantly in the wind as he blew it out slowly.

Briefly and succinctly, he filled Mitch in on what they had learned.

"So," he said to Dan after he had listened in silence. "We have an unknown force of unknown numbers coming for us. They have hostages – potentially – and we don't know where they are based, but we do know they are trained."

"That's about it," Dan said.

"Another glorious day on the farm," Mitch said quietly, mimicking a film Dan couldn't quite place nor did he feel humoured to respond to.

BOXING DAY

"Why do you call it that?" Jan asked Steve quietly as they ate breakfast.

Steve stopped chewing to think.

"No idea to be honest," he said.

"It goes back to the 1700s," said a voice further down the bench to his left. Both men turned to regard the speaker, and both found themselves looking at Mike. Jan did not recognise the man, having never seen him before, but Steve hid his elation well; if that night went as he had hoped, then he would need men like Mike.

"It's something to do with boxing up Christmas gifts," he finished.

"We call it the Day of Goodwill back home," said Jan. "We usually spend it either hungover or getting back on the beers," he finished with a rueful smile.

With an imperceptible nod from Steve, both men finished up their food and rose from the table. Steve accentuated his limp as he passed Mike and muttered that it was good to see him.

The crippled pilot and his once nurse deposited their empty dishes and left the room, swinging by the nearby toilet block. Checking each stall they found it empty and spoke quietly.

"It's Boxing Day for you, my friend" Steve said.

"Is it tonight?" Jan asked Steve excitedly, nervous apprehension twisting his insides. The older man thought for a moment before answering him.

"Yes," Steve answered simply.

A few hundred metres away from the two men who embraced as brothers, two actual brothers spoke quietly.

"Patience," warned Benjamin, who grew tired of his younger brother's eagerness, "in five nights' time, we get our chance."

Will was unhappy at waiting as he had always been, but he had to trust his brother and wait for the right time. They had intentionally rostered the guard duty for New Year's Eve to be light on guards, and encouraged those not working to organise a party. That way most of them would be drunk, and those that remained alert were committed to the brothers' cause.

"Are you planning to fight tonight?" Benjamin asked, having warned his younger brother not to get involved in the underground entertainment and risk injury so close to a crucial time.

"No," the younger man replied forlornly. "I'll just watch and get angry at their incompetence," he said sulkily.

"Good," replied Benjamin, grateful for once that his sibling intended to listen to his advice twice in one day.

END GAME

Steve had arrayed his pieces on the board, he had taken losses and he had stuck to his plan meticulously. He knew the biggest risk to the takeover came from the capable and organized section of the guards, but hoped that Jan's sacrifice – or hopefully *not* sacrifice – would allow for such a diversion that the threat was minimised.

He had visited the window in headquarters where Max, who grew increasingly fearful, had accepted his instructions with as much calm as he could muster. Both Max and Jan were putting themselves in mortal danger without the chance of assistance; all for the greater good.

Now, watching the sun creep downwards in the afternoon sky, he willed the hands on his watch to move faster and bring forward the time for action.

Stepping into the familiar arena with its hard-packed earth and ring of baying onlookers perched high on the ring of shipping containers, Jan felt the change in the crowd as they saw him shirtless for the first time.

He was freezing cold, and his tight skin bristled with goose-bumps. He knew he would warm up very soon, however, as the first challenger stepped in opposite him.

Men cheered, women screeched, and items of worth were wagered on the outcome.

This was the time he had been looking forward to the most. Fuck them. Fuck all of them who think making people fight for their entertainment was good sport. With a final flex of his muscled neck, left and right, he was rewarded with the sounds of cracking as he stepped up and went to work.

His opponent, who he vaguely recognised as either a guard or someone who usually worked outside of the camp walls, came at him head-on without testing him.

Jan waited for the first jab to stab out towards his face and knew from the second the weak punch was thrown that the first fight was already over. Letting the fist come towards his guard he stepped forward and slightly to his right, dropped his body weight, and launched a brutal right-handed punch which connected with the man's torso directly on his liver.

His opponent's forward momentum from the punch carried him onwards as Jan continued to step aside, and his knees had already folded as though he were a puppet with cut strings. Almost unconscious on his feet, the man hit the dirt face first and stayed down.

The crowd erupted with jeers and booing at the poor display, and shouts for another opponent turned into chanting. Guards came forward and dragged the unconscious man away without any regard for causing him further injury.

Far sooner than expected, the second challenger was launched into the arena and the steel door shut behind him like the jaws of a trap. Bigger than Jan and far fatter, he tried to bull-rush the South African and drive him to the dirt. Stepping neatly aside, Jan smacked his fat opponent on the rump making the crowd erupt in laughter.

Twice more he did this, prancing like a bull fighter. On the third attempt, he stood his ground and planted one foot straight onto the exposed shoulder of the man charging him. He dropped like a slaughtered ox and bellowed in pain, trying and failing to regain his feet as the damage to his shoulder was excruciating. Jan stepped to the side of him as he was on all fours, prompting him to look up and beg.

"No! No, please!" he said, before any further pleading was cut short by a savage kick to the back of his head.

Two opponents down in under two minutes. He hated himself a little, but Jan was finally enjoying himself.

The crowd jeered him now for spoiling their entertainment. Cries of "give the next one a chance" rang down to him, and he even heard one woman shout that he was a bully.

What the fuck does she think this is? he thought to himself. *Does she think this is fair?*

Hearing the steel door bang open again and watching as the same two guards now approached, with something resembling a healthy respect for him, and walked forwards to drag the overweight fighter away.

Opponent three was thrust into the ring, and Jan's heart sank.

Kev was scared. He had been okay with being dragged away from his home and the places he liked being. He had felt safe before, carrying the heavy boxes and growing the food, and Maggie looked after him like his mum used to. The men came for him today, and although Maggie screamed at them they took him away. He was put in a room and now they brought him here.

Looking around bewildered, tears stung his eyes because he didn't know what was happening. He was scared. He had seen two men go through the door, had heard lots of shouting which he didn't like, then the two men were carried back past him. Both of them looked hurt, so whatever was outside of that door scared Kev.

Now, realising he was trapped in there with the scary thing, he saw that it was just a man. The man took one look at him then started to shout and swear at the people up on the metal boxes. They laughed at him. They were shouting at Kev now, too. They were telling him to get the man. To hit him. He didn't understand, and he wanted the noise to stop. Chest rising and falling and now in floods of tears, Kev's heart beat so fast he could feel it in his ears. He lined up his sights on the man with no shirt on, and thought that he had to stop him from hurting anyone else.

"You fucking bastards!" screamed Jan, upset and horrified that even these sick people had sunk to such depths that they thought making Kev fight would be amusing. He knew who Kev was, and felt an obligation to him as a caring person – or even as a person with a shred of dignity and even the smallest of hearts – to protect him from this kind of cruelty.

A noise behind him made his chest feel suddenly cold and empty. Turning, he saw Kev, enraged, coming straight at him.

Dodging and throwing himself to the ground he evaded Kev desperately as he rolled back to his feet. Holding out his hands before him he tried to reason with him, tried to tell him to calm down, but he feared from the look on his face that he would hear no reason or explanation.

Hating himself and just about everyone else, he gave up trying to talk Kev down and vowed to end it as quickly as possible without hurting him.

As Kev, incensed and terrified, bore down on him again he stepped to the side as he ducked under a huge swinging forearm and tripped him. Kev landed heavily and bellowed in fear and rage as Jan leapt on his back and forced his face to the dirt again.

Wrapping one strong arm around Kev's neck, he braced the wrist with his free hand and applied pressure to both sides of his neck. He had no intention of choking him, merely trying to interrupt the flow of oxygenated blood to his brain momentarily and put him out. The sickening irony wasn't lost on him that he was trying to replicate the very reason for Kev's disability. Hating himself even more he tightened his grip and shifted his body weight to keep the huge man on the ground.

"Shhh. Shhh," he said involuntarily into Kev's ear, hoping that he would pass out quickly and he could try to forget this ever happened. He could not lose, because the plan wasn't finished yet. He had to win and to put someone he couldn't bring himself to hurt in his path disgusted him. Kev threw back one huge elbow, stinging Jan's eyes and blinding him temporarily with the sheer force of the impact. Jan had to readjust, trapping Kev's hands with his legs one by one to prevent the big man from injuring him.

Feeling Kev's struggles abate slightly, he shifted his grip and squeezed tighter hoping to end it fast.

Kev had other ideas. With a strength Jan didn't think was humanly possible he braced his body and rolled, rising to his feet and carrying Jan's not insubstantial weight with him as though he were made of air and freeing one hand in the process. Jan buried his unprotected eyes into the back of Kev's shoulder, fearful of the big hand flailing at him but still not releasing his grip one ounce, as he tried to hang on.

With a strangled bellow, Kev instinctively threw himself backwards. Driving every breath of air from Jan's lungs as their combined weight slammed into the hard ground, he felt his head crack against the earth. Dizzy and winded, Jan used every bit of muscle strength he could muster to maintain his grip.

Slowly, with sounds coming from Kev which broke his heart, the struggling stopped and the big man went limp.

Shrugging his huge weight off him, Jan struggled to his feet, eyes full of tears, and checked Kev's vital signs.

He was breathing, but unconscious. Shouting for help he saw the door bang open again and the same guards walking towards him with undisguised fear in their eyes this time; not only were they fearful of Jan who had dispatched three fighters in as many minutes, but they were fearful of the beast waking up and killing them. With difficulty, Kev was carried from the arena with Jan following and shouting at them to keep his neck supported. At the exit, a rifle barrel was prodded into his chest and he stepped back for the door to close.

Breathing heavily like he had finished a sprint, he cuffed away his tears of remorse and disgust for what he had just had to do, and looked at the faces of the spectators.

They jeered, they laughed, they pointed, they wagered.

All except one.

Singling him out with a pointed finger, Jan shouted.

"You," he bawled, gaining the attention of most of the onlookers. "Was that your idea?"

Will smirked and shrugged. If he wasn't allowed to fight, then the least he could do was be allowed to watch the massive simpleton beat other people to death.

"Coward!" Jan screamed, then spat towards him. His eyes never left Will's face.

The crowd loved it. A personal challenge to one of the best. This was real holiday entertainment.

Will made a move to climb down from the raised seating until the man next to him grabbed his arm.

"Benjamin said not to fight!" hissed Will's co-conspirator. "Stick to the plan!"

Will snatched his arm clear from the man and climbed down, happy to ignore his brother's orders but pathologically unable to resist a direct challenge.

The crowd roared with anticipation as Jan desperately tried to get his breath back. All feeling of the cold night evaporated as Will stepped into the arena.

And smiled.

CHECK

Steve's chosen few fell in step with him as he strode through the shadows towards the nearest weapons locker. By now, others were passing word around that they were about to rise. To wait to be given guns and to be ready to overthrow Richards. No longer accentuating his limp, he walked tall and strong towards the two guards standing by a metal container.

"Drink, Sir?" Max said, holding aloft an expensive bottle which he knew was to Richards's tastes. He had intercepted it from a delivery intended for the very same office, but the Major had no idea. Things just appeared for him, and he liked that.

"Good man!" he exclaimed, dropping his pen and pulling a sheet of paper to cover his work. He beckoned the young man inside.

Max had been preparing himself for this moment, but it was all he could do to keep the bile from rising in his throat.

Stepping past the chair Richards offered him with an outstretched hand, he walked around to the other side of the desk and sat delicately on the edge. Pouring two glasses, measures which any bar would call at least a triple, he gave Richards one glass and raised his own.

"Cheers," he said with what he hoped was his cheekiest smile.

Richards blushed and drank, pulling a face as the fierce liquid hit his throat. Catching a glimpse of the paperwork which Richards had hastily tried to cover, Max leaned over his shoulder and moved it aside.

"Sir," he said chidingly, "you never told me you were so talented!" Richards blushed a deeper shade of red and mumbled something about always having been an artist at heart, but Max wasn't interested in his words. He pulled out the paper and made admiring noises about what he would only describe as a child's drawing.

Placing a hand on Richards's shoulder, Max told him that he was wasted as a senior officer in the army and should've been an artist.

The incorrect inflation of Richards's former rank combined with the compliment had the desired effect.

Max refilled Richards's glass twice as he listened to the man waffle on about how his passion for sketching had started at an early age.

So flattered was he that this young man was taking a personal interest in him, that Richards failed to notice he was still drinking the first drink he had poured himself, and that the bottle was already a third empty.

Glancing surreptitiously at his watch, Max smiled and hoped to god that the next hour would pass quickly.

~

Standing face to face with Will for the second time in the arena, Jan felt a rage inside him like never before. Even when mentally preparing to fight the bastard without making himself lose like last time, he had no way of summoning such anger than he felt at that moment.

"You think that was *sport?*" he snapped at Will, unable to control himself as his voice cracked with anger.

Will said nothing. His calm arrogance infuriated Jan and forced him to strike first.

Lashing out with his left foot straight at his chest, Will stepped back and to the side like Jan knew he would. As soon as his left foot hit the ground, his right shot out in a savage round kick which Will had no chance of avoiding. Blocking it with both hands braced, the force knocked him backwards to the ground making the crowd erupt in a higher octave than before.

Rolling effortlessly backwards and regaining his feet without his hands touching the ground, he smiled again.

Jan had, in his own words, totally lost his shit. He fired attack after attack at Will, making the younger man dodge and block all over the arena until, far too quickly, Jan was blown.

He had made a fundamental mistake, and he had winded himself. Will was not only younger and lighter, but he was also fresh to the fight and he knew it. Jan was almost doubled over, desperately sucking in air to replenish the oxygen expended from his body, and Will chose that moment to counter. Raining kicks and punches into Jan's body if he protected his head, and into his head if he protected his body, Will still smiled as he landed blow after blow on the exhausted man.

After maybe ten hits, Jan's hands dropped involuntarily and he took harder blows as Will pressed his obvious advantage. Switching tactics as Jan knew he would, Will surprised him with a savage attack as he came in close but instead of throwing his fists into him he spun elegantly under his arms and gripped his chest from behind. Powerless to prevent it, Jan felt his body lift upwards as Will twisted and slammed his head, neck and shoulders into the dirt. Before he could even tell which way was up, his breath caught in his throat as Will's arm slid over his shoulder and around his neck. Reacting instantly, instinctively, Jan dropped his chin to his chest and shrugged his shoulders, shooting his left hand across his body to grab Will's right. Rolling to his left he only narrowly avoided Will securing the choke hold. Continuing the roll to escape and create distance, Jan's failing strength hurt him as the younger, faster and fresher man landed two punches in quick succession to his face just as he regained his feet.

Wavering on the spot like a punch-drunk boxer who was overdue to retire, Jan stood in the centre of the arena and waited for his fortune to be read.

From the ranks of baying onlookers he heard one voice shout, "Finish him!" in mockery of a video game.

Will cracked at that point, and laughed.

That sound, that infuriating sound, cut through Jan's consciousness like a knife.

Will stepped forward and lined up a show-boat of a spinning kick which he knew would please his audience. He pivoted and his head whipped backwards as he momentarily took his eyes off his target, Jan summoned his remaining strength and launched himself forward, placing all his effort into his outstretched right foot.

Will spun back, his eyes widening as he realised Jan was no longer where he ought to be, just as the boot connected with his straight left leg.

There was no room for manoeuvre. No give in that bracing leg, and the momentum of the weight behind Jan's foot continued straight through the joint and issued a sickening crunch which was drowned out by the crowd.

Will, one leg bent backwards in a grotesque way nature did not intend, slumped to the ground unable to breathe through the pain, instantly silencing the crowd.

Staggering towards the younger man clawing at his ruined leg, Jan leaned down.

And smiled.

Not a word rang out. The crowd watched in stunned horror and Will held one hand out towards his attacker as the other gripped his ruined knee. Jan seized that hand in a vice-like grip around the wrist, rolled backwards and wrapped his legs around Will's neck, hooking one leg over the other foot.

Bracing his body with every single ounce of strength remaining in him, he tensed and rolled back. Will emitted a single squawk of agony until the pressure around his neck prevented anything else, then his eyes bulged and spit bubbled at his mouth. His face flushed purple, but he made no attempt to extricate himself. The strength of Jan's hold on him dragged the younger man upright where he pulled the arms and crushed his neck with his thighs. Weakly, feebly, Will's free hand fluttered at Jan's leg in a form of submission.

Jan ignored the futile gesture.

With a final heave of brute force Jan wrenched Will's head sideways and upwards, twisting his whole body with the last of his might, and received a satisfying 'pop' from Will's neck.

Shoving the limp body off him, he struggled to his feet once more, filled his lungs, and bellowed out all his rage and anger.

The man who had tried to stop Will from fighting had already left the arena in a dead sprint to find Benjamin.

SIEGE PART I

Dawn and dusk. The two times that every soldier, every person who has ever seen warfare, is at their most alert; the two times of the day when attacks seem to be universally planned.

Modern tactics and good sense progressed to attacks in darkness during the dead hours when everyone would ordinarily be asleep or too tired to respond to threat quickly.

Being far from a classic soldier in many senses, le chasseur ordered his troops into position before dawn and ordered them to wait, hidden, until midday when he believed that most people would be ignorant of any risk and thinking about food. His main force was five miles out, hidden in a gully which offered protection from sight. They had the British military vehicle which Sabine had taken, and they would use that to best effect after the door was opened.

His own group, a hand-picked force of six, crept forwards before the sun rose to the agreed place.

If his plan had not worked, if the weak Frenchman failed him, then they still had a plan B and C before he signalled for an aborted mission.

Much to his vicious delight, he found the rope hanging almost exactly where he had wanted it, giving his elite vanguard the shortest climb possible to the fort. Having moved as stealthily as possible over rough ground in the dark he knew they would all be tired, so he ordered a short rest before they ascended the rope.

A climb of thirty feet up a vertical wall put immense pressure on the upper body strength of the men which was another reason he had chosen the men behind him. Leading from the front as ever, he left his heavier equipment at the base of the wall for retrieval later, and began to climb.

Muscles burning and the breath rasping in his throat, he eventually placed one hand over the lip of the rough stone and followed it with the other. Raising his eyes over the parapet, he saw one man. The man was asleep with his back to a wall as he sat, and Leo's disgust at the lack of professionalism stung him. A sentry unable to hear a man climbing only feet away was an insult to him.

Recognising the man as the one he had recruited to make their silent infiltration possible made his disgust no less evident; this man even knew to expect them. Leaning over and beckoning up the next man, his implacable sniper, he crept low to the sleeping man and placed a hand over his mouth.

Waking with a start, Olivier regarded him with wide eyes until logic overtook fear. When Leo knew the man would not cry out, he removed his hand and spoke to him in hushed French.

"Help the others up, and well done, solider," he said with a smile dripping with insincerity.

The man didn't notice, he just seemed pathetically pleased to be part of something. To be accepted by a man he clearly envied and wanted to emulate: his new master.

One by one the other legionnaires gained the high ground in deathly silence and took big lungfulls of air to begin the day's work.

"How many up here?" he asked Olivier.

"Six," he replied, "and me."

Seven to kill then, thought Leo.

Drawing his knife and waiting for his soldiers to follow suit, he crept into the darkness.

One by one, the sleeping guards of the sky fort died.

Leo killed two himself. One young man, asleep on his back, woke to see the snarling Frenchman leaning over him, hand clamped across his mouth, and the long drive inched slowly between his ribs to penetrate the heart. Le chasseur was enjoying himself, and he took a sick pleasure in watching the man's life fade away from his eyes.

The last man, the only one awake, stood and watched the glow of the sky from his position overlooking the road. An impressive rifle was slung over his right shoulder, but such a distance weapon was useless. He may as well have been carrying a stick for all the good it did him.

Approaching him from the shadows behind like a cat stalking prey, Leo rose and drew the wicked edge of the blade across the left side of his neck and pressed harder as he opened the windpipe to prevent any noise he might make.

Catching his body as he fell back, he watched the man spasm and die like a landed fish. His men watched his smile without betraying any emotion, but Olivier stood open-mouthed in horror.

"Strip the bodies," he ordered him, "and dump them over the wall where we climbed up."

Olivier did as he was told, struggling with the dead weight of each man as he dragged them by their feet or hands to the ramparts leaving trails of blood to mark his progress. Each man was stripped of equipment, and Olivier took their personal possessions without any shame.

When the last body was ready to be hauled over the side, before he heard the now familiar sound of silence ending with a crunching, wet thump, Leo reappeared flanked by two of his men.

"I will help you with that one," he said, surprising the smaller man.

The two of them lifted the body, and Leo leaned over with a smile to watch it fall like a rag doll to the pile of broken bodies below.

"Look at that!" he said to Olivier, who leaned over out of some automatic obedience.

As he did, the two men behind him stepped forwards and lifted a leg each, pitching him over the side.

Desperately Olivier spun and scrabbled for safety, managing to turn his body and grip the stone ledge. The rough surface cut into his soft hands painfully as he stared at Leo with pleading eyes.

Leo left him there, dangling, and smiled wider.

"You know," he said, "if there's one thing I cannot abide, it's a traitor."

With that, he drew his knife and sliced deep cuts across the backs of Olivier's hands.

The tendons and ligaments irreparably damaged, Olivier's grip failed and he dropped into the wind-rushing silence of the void.

⸍

"I do not like it, Englishman," said Pietro testily. He had joined Dan on the wall above the gate by the big machine gun.

"There is bad in the air," he finished.

Dan, perplexed at the superstitious air about the big Russian, asked for elaboration.

"It is, how you say, the other senses?" he said questioningly.

"Like a sixth sense?" Dan asked him.

"Exactly this," Pietro replied, failing to expand any further.

It worried Dan, because he had failed to trust instincts before. He had ignored his own and almost died. He had ignored Ash's and almost died along with Leah and two others. He felt uneasy ignoring the instincts of the big game hunter by his side, but he did not feel the same sense of foreboding which was troubling the man now.

The Russian walked away, but Dan noticed he wore his own unique version of full battle gear; the wolf pelt, a quiver brimming with feathered arrows and likely more blades than a butcher's shop.

Dan, similarly dressed in a fashion, wore his customary black clothing with his heavy body armour. On the back, trusty as ever but rarely used, sat the brute of a shotgun and the front of his chest was festooned with spare magazines for his new assault rifle and silenced sidearm. Ash, wearing nothing but his mottled grey fur, was always dressed for battle.

He stood there, immovable and implacable, until the sun rose. Pietro's uneasiness had been infectious, and he now began to sense that something was amiss.

Picking up one radio set, he checked in with the tower high up on his left side. All clear.

Picking up the other, he checked in with the fort.

Silence.

Trying again, using a more urgent voice as is the way of people using communications, he hailed them again.

"All clear," came the gruff response after a pause.

Sighing with relief, a small amount of the pressure lifted from his shoulders, he relaxed.

Five miles away, at the agreed time, two men were unbound and dragged to their feet. Both seemed broken, but the taller man's dark skin was swollen and bruised.

A man stepped forward to the smaller one and dragged him a short distance away. Opening his heavy coat given to him to protect him from the elements, the man connected a wire to the batteries strapped to the vest under the coat, lifted his right hand, and squeezed it easily around the ball and trigger switch. Putting a single piece of loose sticky tape over his fingers, he let the hand fall and connected another wire running down the other sleeve.

"You remember what to do?" he asked him quietly in English.

"Yes," replied Chris, woodenly and with unfocussed eyes.

"When you see the gate, click the other switch to arm it," said the Frenchman, receiving a nod of understanding.

Turning away, he ordered the other man to be brought up as he zipped up Chris' heavy coat.

"Walk," they were ordered, the way to the road being pointed out to them.

Chris and Simon began walking towards Sanctuary.

CHECKMATE

Benjamin heard the news, but did not have time to process it. His man had run to him when Will had first stepped in the arena, so neither knew the violent and gruesome result of the fight yet, but both ran to the ring of shipping containers with desperate purpose.

They needed Will for their plans in just a few days' time, and even more so after that, and they needed him even more after that. Having him injured now would be a foolish waste of an opportunity that they had staked their lives on.

A massive commotion met them as they neared the arena. Barging through the single entry door, Benjamin emerged out to see Jan being guarded at gunpoint. The two guards seemed unsure of what to do, and more and more people flocked to the crowd to see what had happened.

The relief was evident on the faces of some as Benjamin could finally give coherent orders, but most viewed him with a strange look of frightened anticipation.

Looking past the shirtless man on his knees, he saw a body slumped on the ground. It was clear to Benjamin that the way the body lay indicated that they would never get up, and his worst fears materialised into reality as he stepped nearer.

His brother lay face down at his feet, one leg bent backwards at the knee. He barely breathed, and Benjamin was too frightened to move him and injure him further.

"Who did this?" he asked pointlessly, prompting everyone around him to glance at one another hoping that they would not be the bearer of bad news.

Turning to face the guards covering the kneeling man, one of them wordlessly pointed at him.

Looking at the man's face for the first time, he saw him smiling.

Drawing a sidearm in one smooth motion he braced one leg back and took a two-handed aim at the man's forehead with tears pricking his eyes.

A single shot rang out, but not from Benjamin's gun. Confusion called for a moment's silence, before another shot tore the air from the other side of the camp.

As one, the guards and Benjamin ran from the arena; vengeance for his brother's injuries temporarily forgotten.

Jan, still breathing heavily from the fight and his expected death, slumped to the ground and lay on his back.

Looking over to his left, the outstretched hand of Will was near his own. Slapping it weakly, Jan lay back and muttered to himself.

"High five, bro."

Steve and his group of militants rounded the corner and came face to face with the two bored sentries stood by the weapons locker.

They were startled by the appearance of him, but their confusion evaporated when the others came into view and their weapons came up to point at the intruders.

"Just listen for a second," Steve said, holding his open hands up. "Richards has to go, we all know it. Join us, please."

One man hesitated, his aim wavering, before he dropped the barrel of his rifle to point at the floor. Standing up, he turned to the other guard.

"It's not worth dying for," he said simply.

The other guard's response was to shoot him, point blank, in the chest.

Steve dived for the fallen rifle of the dead man before it hit the floor, but as he saw the guard switch his aim and fire a second harmless round, which miraculously missed everyone, a shape stepped quickly from the shadows and flashed a bright reflection across the man's neck.

Dropping to his knees, blood bubbling at his throat, Lizzie walked slowly into the light with a bloodied scalpel in her shaking hand.

Steve lay on the floor with the rifle half aimed towards the dying man, and made eye contact with Lizzie.

"I knew it," she said, almost triumphantly, as though trying to ignore the fact that she had just cut a man's throat. "I knew you'd be involved in this somehow."

Climbing to his feet, seeing the shock in her eyes that he stood tall and strong, he hugged her tightly.

"Lizzie," he muttered in her ear, "I've been planning this from the second I woke up here."

Withdrawing from each other, Steve rapidly opened the locker using a key found in the bloody pocket of the guard Lizzie had killed and began issuing weapons. Others were emerging from the shadows now, falling in line to be armed.

Steve felt like a Russian army officer in the siege of Stalingrad. He had no idea why the imagery from a film seen long ago came to him then, but he thanked whatever higher power that looked down on them that he was issuing guns to everyone, and not having to give one person a gun and the next a clip of spare ammunition.

The first shouts of alarm were punctuated by the sounds of incoming fire from the rush of guards heading their way.

Barking orders, Steve organised his guerrilla forces into the dark alleyways of the camp, knowing that this fight could rage throughout the night.

The sounds of gunfire silenced the giggles in Richards's office. Max had managed to get him to drink almost half of the bottle now, pretending to be getting drunk with him as he suffered the boring vitriol which the man spouted.

When the first shot rang out, closely followed by a second, Richards stood with a wobble and retrieved a sidearm from the top drawer of his desk. Snatching up two spare magazines, he shoved them into his pocket as he tried to walk around the desk but bumped his leg into it heavily.

Max jumped to his feet, forgetting to pretend he had matched the man measure for measure, and stood to block the doorway.

"Probably just some of the lads getting carried away celebrating!" he said with a false smile.

"Carried away?" Richards slurred, taking a step backwards to steady himself.

He closed one eye to focus better, and used the gun in his hand to emphasise his words, unintentionally pointing it at Max's chest.

"*Carried away?*" he snarled. "Young man, there is never an excuse for a soldier to discharge his firearm for any reason other than training or during hostilities," he said arrogantly, making Max believe he was quoting some old rule book on the correct conduct for soldiers at war.

Max opened his mouth to protest further but was interrupted by further shots.

He glanced to the window, as though the inky blackness outside could provide an answer, and turned back to find the gun pointed in his face.

"You're part of this, aren't you?" Richards said, sobering up.

Max stammered in answer until the pistol barrel whipped across his cheek and knocked him to the ground in agony.

Scrabbling backwards he held his hands in front of his face and begged for Richards to stop. Blood already ran down his face and he could feel the hot wetness of it as the metallic smell hit his nostrils.

"Please, sir, no!" he said, tucking himself into a ball as Richards aimed two wild kicks at his body.

"This is a coup!" he screeched.

"YES!" yelled Max, stopping the next kick before it landed.

"It's Benjamin," he said through tears, "and Will. They threatened my family and said they would kill me if I told you. I tried to keep you here so they wouldn't hurt you."

The lie, smoothly told under the extreme circumstances, performed perfectly.

Richards staggered back, as though physically wounded by the news, but was touched by the false sentiment.

"You care about me?" he asked in disbelief. "You tried to save my life?"

"Yes, sir," said Max, snivelling as he regained his feet.

Richards stepped forward and pulled the young man into a tight embrace.

Max, in his fear and inexperience, then made a mistake.

He reached for the gun as he soothed the man. Richards felt the pressure on the weapon and gripped it tighter. Max tried to pull it away from him. The two men locked eyes and Richards knew with absolute certainty then that Max was lying to him. He was part of it.

Baring his teeth he pulled the gun away harder as he disengaged from the younger man. Max held on.

The report of the weapon, muffled in the tight confines between their bodies, still deafened him. The flash from the muzzle still blinded him momentarily, and the stench of cordite stung his eyes. He watched as Max's eyes went wide, as his mouth opened and closed twice, then let him fall to the ground and watched as the red circle of his white shirt widened until it covered his whole abdomen.

Richards stood over the dying boy and said nothing. Wordlessly he walked to the large, ornate mirror in his office and straightened his collar and regarded his appearance for a few minutes. Satisfied that the Major looked his best, he stepped over the body and opened the door to face the threat head on.

The fight did not last long. Steve had an organized group, although many were untrained, and the guards were in disarray. He had lined his rebels, his freedom fighters, behind a low barricade and cut down the reactionary force of guards easily. They were ill-trained, poorly led and utterly confused.

As he ordered people to move positions in groups, the fighting condensed towards the building designated as headquarters where they met a stalemate. The heavy gun positions, in relative safety on the higher ground of the steps and surrounded by sandbags, rained fire on anyone who showed their faces in the open. Guards loyal to the cause, or at least confused as to whose side they should be on, trickled in to the defended position.

The approach could not be flanked, and neither would any side agree to parlay.

Steve had to break the deadlock quickly, or face an uncertain outcome.

"You, you and you. Come with me," he said, picking out three men who he had seen handle their weapons competently. "Everyone else, stay hidden and keep them busy with occasional shots. Don't let them get organized and flank you."

Jogging around the building, they followed him to the low window which he pushed open and climbed inside. Treading mud and blood onto Max's clean bed, they filed into the room and prepared to break out into the corridors. They were in the enemy's rear, and they had to finish it.

Snaking through the rooms they heard the noise of the gunfire increase as they neared the main entrance.

Creeping towards the door, Steve ducked back into cover as Richards's office opened and the man himself strode out to the exit.

Steve followed, stopping abruptly as his peripheral vision caught a pair of legs and a pool of blood.

He couldn't look at the body, but he knew who it would be and he knew, with absolute certainty, that the boy's death was on him. He had enough blood on his hands already, but that sacrifice was entirely his doing. Leaving that demon to be exorcised some other time, he went for the door.

~

Benjamin was staying low behind the sandbags and calling targets out to his few remaining troops. Of those with him, he had maybe half which were loyal to the brothers. Or, as he thought in anguish, to the brother. If he could quell this uprising, then Richards could still be overthrown and he could salvage at least something from the day. As he worked, the door burst open behind him.

Richards strode up to him, anger on his face and blood on his uniform.

"Sir," he began, but never finished the sentence.

Raising his gun, Richards shot Benjamin once in the neck and watched with satisfaction as he fell.

The firing stopped, and the loyalty of the traitors was tested.

It failed, almost instantly, and as one they turned their attention back to the threat ahead ever backing the status quo.

Steve looked at the three men with him. He pointed first to himself and then pointed straight forwards through the exit. He pointed to the next man and pointed left, the man after and pointed right.

He burst through the door, opening the clasp first then gripping his weapon as he used his shoulder to widen the gap. Spraying the gun positions from the rear on full auto he carried on stepping forwards. Behind him, the others came out spraying and within seconds the fight was over.

And they had won.

Richards, wounded but too enraged to feel the pain, saw his nemesis lower his weapon and walk forwards. He saw Steve shout but didn't hear the words, and simply lay still planning his next move. His final act of vengeance.

Rising to his feet, he heard shouts of alarm.

Steve stood at the top of the stone steps, but in the dusk not the dawn as his recurring dream had been. He saw faces in the crowd smiling at him. He saw people he recognized, people he didn't know as well as those he knew well.

Lizzie shouldered her way through the front rank and ran to him. He dropped his rifle into the dirt and gripped her tightly in an embrace which seemed to convey everything he felt. His gratitude for her saving his life, his fears and worries of the last months living under the tyrannical rule of a madman, his relief that it was all, finally, over.

Just then a scream sounded, followed by a cry of alarm, and he turned to look up at Richards pointing a gun at him.

The gun raised in slow motion. He saw the barrel rise, was powerless to do anything about it, and stood transfixed by the black circle of the business end of the gun and waited for the flash.

Unlike in his recurring nightmare, he didn't wait for the flash. He closed his eyes and accepted his fate, believing that he had achieved something worthwhile. He almost welcomed his death, as though martyrdom could wash away all the blood on his hands and erase the memory of the terrible things he had seen and done.

He saw no flash, but he heard the bang.

SIEGE PART 2

The opening of any attack is always assumed to be big. An overwhelming show of force, the launching of an offensive designed to force the enemy into death or submission.

This attack followed a different script.

Two lone figures wandered staggering into view on the road. Betraying the alertness and concentration of Claude in the watchtower who had the smallest of angles in his favour, the radio crackled to life seconds before Dan saw them on the road.

He assumed that the fort would have seen the approach sooner, but he had no time to question their silence.

From the distance they were seen at, and judging by the rate at which they walked, he guessed they would be there inside of three minutes.

"Should we sound the alarm?" Leah asked, cool and collected on the outside but screaming inside.

"Not yet," Dan replied. "They could be from the farm." Ash whined at his side as though he knew that Dan didn't wholly believe his own words.

The two men didn't speak as they trudged down the road. Chris gasped when the town walls came into view, and fumbled with his left hand. Simon watched what he did, trying to work out a logical reason in his sleep-starved brain as to why he had sticky tape on the hand he pulled from his pocket. Walking towards what he thought was safe as though in a waking dream filled with torment, the questions bouncing around in his head couldn't hold his concentration long enough to materialise into words.

Chris' eyes stayed resolutely on the gates. He had a job to do. He had a destiny. Everything was Dan's fault and nobody could stop him but Chris. He only knew that to stop him hurting anyone else, he had to follow his instructions.

"It's his fault," he mumbled, waking Simon from the trance he had lapsed back into.

"What?" he said, more confused than questioning.

"It's Dan's fault. Everything is," Chris replied in an emotionless voice.

"What did he do?" Simon asked, out of curiosity more than reason, not fully remembering who Dan was or what he had done to be blamed.

"It's his fault," Chris said again, not even understanding his own logic but merely repeating the same mantra he had tattooed on his brain for weeks.

Simon thought, which was almost impossible as his brain had given up making the connections it used to.

"Dan was good to me," he said. The statement was almost a question as he spoke it aloud uncertainly.

"He... He saved me?" he finished.

Chris stopped walking.

"It's his fault," he said with tears in his eyes. "My baby died and it's his fault."

Simon stopped and looked at him.

"But he was good to me," he said, slightly more sure of his answer this time.

A shout came from the shapes of the people above the gateway, above the archway blocked by the heavy wooden doors. Neither of the men responded, both regarding each other uncertainly.

Simon grabbed the heavy coat Chris wore by the chest with both hands and pulled him towards his face.

"He was good to me!" he said savagely, like an aggressive drunk with no idea why he was angry. Chris' hands came up to his face, and Simon saw something. He didn't know what it was, and couldn't make sense of it, but he knew – more like *felt* – that it was horribly, terribly wrong.

Chris' left palm held a switch with a faint red light under the letters A/C.

His right hand gripped a silver ball tightly, the sticky tape now gone.

Something else felt wrong, and Simon struggled against Chris' weak hands to pull down the zip. His senses returned to him, only slightly, but enough to recognize what he saw. The term 'suicide vest' sprang into his mind, recalled from a news bulletin from a different life, and he let go.

Turning back to the gate, he tried to shout a warning but no words came. Chris shoved him hard, using his shoulder to drive him to the ground, and ran for the gate.

He ran, although shambled would have been a better description. Reaching the gateway, he looked up and saw the face above him.

Drawing in his ragged breath he yelled, "It's your fault," and released the pressure in his right hand.

Dan saw the two men approaching. He saw them stop, and saw the taller man grab the smaller one by the chest. He saw the smaller man shove the other to the ground and run, as though injured or drunk, towards him.

Leah wasted no time, nor did she wait for permission. Turning and raising her weapon towards the sea she took careful aim and fired a single shot. Her bullet hit the bell in the nearby tower, only a glancing blow but enough for the metallic sound to ring out. That sound picked up in volume and intensity as the boy posted below it hauled on the rope with all his might. The alarm was raised, and the townspeople would now be scrambling to their positions of either safety or defence.

As the bell began to ring, Dan leaned over and saw the face of Chris looking up at him. The savagery, the pure hatred on his face, made Dan feel cold inside. He could see military drab colours beneath a big coat, and as the words he shouted reached him he raised his own weapon and loosed a single shot.

The response to his shot, fired on pure instinct without any logic behind it, was answered with such destruction that he had no idea what had happened. The three satchel charges strapped to Chris' chest detonated, only split seconds apart, but with the effect of one huge explosion.

As the bullet dropped Chris, its high-angled trajectory driving down through his shoulder and into his ribcage, he pitched backwards. The shaped charges, which a second before would have torn down the side of the archway, now projected upwards along the face of the wall.

Chris disintegrated. He didn't blow apart, he simply vanished. One moment he was there, the next he wasn't. In his place was a blossoming gout of dark black smoke.

The blast tore huge lumps of stone from the wall and shook a thousand years of compacted dust from the crevices. Dan was blown backwards but the force of the explosion carried on vertically upwards, shaped by the ancient wall. Barely conscious and with such a high-pitched ringing in his ears, he lay on his back as everything turned white with the cascading dust which swirled in the wind. He replayed the scene in his head, frame by frame, seeing the horrific moment when a man who was his friend vanished in a cloud of red-tinted black smoke, dust and stone.

He had no idea how badly damaged he was, and his first thought was to search for Ash and Leah. All around him lumps of stone rained down. He was oblivious to the pain of those which hit him.

He shouted their names, unable to hear anything but the screeching in his ears and head as he tried to roll and blink away the grit in his eyes. The stench of the explosion stung his throat. The cloying, sickening chemical smell of the blast seemed to stick to everything.

Leah ran to him. He watched as she dropped to her knees in slow motion and shouted his name. He could read her lips, but could not hear the sound of her voice. Ash, tail tucked desperately between his legs and almost curling into a ball on his feet circled desperately, terrified of the noise and the sight of his master hurt. He was struck by the thought that Ash was lucky he had run with Leah to raise the alarm, as that put them both out of reach of the blast.

His mind raced like that, detached, as the world continued to move in silent slow motion around him under the incessant soundtrack of the ringing noise which seemed to ebb and flow in intensity.

Leah's deft hands checked down his body, evidently finding nothing of any great concern, as she took hold of the tough loop on his vest at the base of his neck. With some difficulty, she dragged him clear of the rubble towards the stairs leading down.

Still unable to hear any words, he watched as she yelled orders and pointed people into position.

Dan, as much as he hated to admit it, would probably have to sit the rest of this one out.

~

Simon watched from fifty paces away as Chris ran to the gate. He heard a shot, then sat unmoving on the stony ground as the man he had just walked with disappeared in a maelstrom of destruction. The dust from the blast was snatched away by the wind, and he stared in horror as part of the wooden gateway fell inwards to leave a hole into the lightless interior.

Already in terrible physical condition, his body screamed at him from the hot pressure wave of the blast. Every internal organ seemed to have been rocked by the impossibly sharp crack of the explosion.

The explosion had served to return at least some of his understanding, but he still sat and stared at the carnage in front of him.

Fearing the small part of what had just happened that he could understand, he slowly struggled to his feet and began removing his clothes until he was certain he wasn't a walking bomb as Chris had been. Logic and sense evaporated as the thick, black smoke began to clear, but Simon couldn't comprehend that even his boots weren't explosives. Stripping to a filthy t-shirt and underwear, his mind returned to the present.

The silence faded back into noise as the sound of a bell ringing frantically drifted to him on the wind. The wind changed direction, swirling in the ravine of the road, and the sound of the bell was replaced by the muted sound of a diesel engine.

~

Mitch made it to the ramparts first, with Pietro close behind him. Leah looked ashen, but her eyes ringed red with stone dust and tears.

Gaining the top step, he looked at the supine form of Dan, turned white by the same dust, and unconscious. Blood ran from his right ear, thickening and creeping down his neck as it mingled with the dust.

Turning to Pietro, the Russian seemed to understand Mitch's question before it came. Snatching up the man on the floor, he turned around and began to descend the stairs with him held in his arms like a sleeping child.

"They bombed the gates!" Leah told him desperately. "They bombed the fucking gates, with a person!" she yelled, as though trying to make sense of what had just happened.

Mitch was not new to this concept. He had trained for hours, years even, to deal with bomb threats. Homemade grenades thrown over the walls of barracks in Northern Ireland. Rocket propelled grenade attacks in Iraq and Afghanistan.

And suicide bombers.

The simple fact, with so few people left alive, that anyone would resort to such cruel and evil tactics shocked him but the process did not. He had seen it too many times.

He also knew that this would not be the only attack.

Running to the ramparts where, blessedly, only a small section of wall was down, he breathed an internal sigh of relief as the gun was still in place. Ten paces further away was where Dan had been, but the big machine gun still stood, and could still spit fire and death towards the enemy.

An enemy which now came.

Ripping away the tarpaulin, he wrenched back the huge handle to chamber a massive round into the breech and sighted along the long, perforated barrel to see a vehicle coming into view.

The sheer audacity of it made his blood boil.

They, the bastards, were attacking them using their own damned armoured truck. As the Foxhound lined up straight towards the gate, he put the start of the pressure on the firing switch and prepared to fire bursts of heavy calibre bullets into the approaching vehicle and the people jogging alongside it.

Just at that moment, before the firing pin hit the first round, another bullet on a different trajectory took the flesh off the top of his right shoulder.

~

"Hit," said the Frenchman in the fort to Leo who stood over his shoulder.

"Good," came the reply. "Keep them off that gun and our forces will walk through the door.

The sniper didn't respond. He had his job, and anything showing on that rampart would be the next to take his bullet.

~

A clear kilometre away and late to the party due to a gross underestimation of the rough ground he had to cover, a solitary legionnaire finally crested the mountain top and took cover to observe the back of the watchtower. Waiting to regain his breath, he heard – *felt* – the sound of the explosion and knew he was far behind schedule.

Rushing, and ignoring his own safety for fear of displeasing his commanding officer, he kicked down the door to find the ground floor empty. Lowering his gun, he heard the sounds of creaking floorboards above and simply waited for the person to come into view. He fired a burst of rounds and watched in satisfaction as a body fell down the remaining steps. Exhausted, he slumped into a rocking chair to catch his breath before taking up overwatch.

Claude, for all his advancing years, moved like a cat. On hearing the door burst open two floors below him, he quietly shimmied down the external wooden ladder and circled back to the entrance.

The man sat down panting had no prelude to his death; had no indication that he was finished. The bullet entered the back of his head and exited through his eye socket, embedding itself into a thick wooden beam opposite.

"That's my wife's chair," said Claude.

~

"Mitch!" screamed Leah from her prone position tucked under the lip of the wall as she tried to make herself as small as possible.

The soldier gritted his teeth and growled like an animal over and over as he tried to force the pain away. With his left hand clamped onto the gaping wound with blood seeping through his fingers, he shuffled himself into better cover as best he could. Leah crawled towards him, just as Ash barked and began to come to her.

"No!" she screamed, pointing towards the archway to the staircase. "Back!"

Ash, confused and scared, nonetheless did as he was told and slinked off down the steps.

Reaching behind her right shoulder she took out a compression bandage without looking, clamping the dressing pad with its coagulating power onto the wound and wrapping the elasticated bandage tightly over it and around the upper arm. Tying it off with the built-in tourniquet in seconds, the two locked eyes.

"I need the battery and the command wire," he said to her, the pain evident on his face.

Nodding, Leah crawled over his towards the gun and retrieved the battery, sliding it towards him. Scrabbling with her hands in the dust and stone fragments she searched desperately for the copper wire. Just behind her right foot, a chunk of stone the size of an apple disappeared and it sounded to her like another explosion had gone off just behind her.

With a scream she withdrew into a tiny ball, her slung rifle scraping noisily on the stone. She stayed there, covering her head with both hands still clutching the copper wire.

"Sniper," said Mitch pointlessly. "Got our range. Stay low," he reassured her.

Slowly, mastering her fear, Leah began to crawl back to him. Two other shots sounded, the echoing crash of the supersonic metal hitting ancient stone reverberating around the ramparts and terrifying her.

Handing the wire to him, he carefully kept the copper away from the battery. Now came the hardest part.

"I need to know when the vehicle is at the flag," he told her.

Nothing more needed to be said.

Turning her position around so she squatted in front of the wall, she popped up like a demented jack in the box and dropped immediately, a fraction of a second before the answering bullet flew in her direction. Another involuntary scream escaped her mouth and she huddled down, trying to control her breathing.

"Close," she panted, voice cracking. "Not yet."

"Change position," Mitch said, his whole right arm now numb from the compression bandage and the gaping hole in his flesh underneath that.

Scraping herself three paces until she neared the gun, she stopped. To go further meant to go around the legs of the weapon, and that would expose her to the deadly fire.

Squatting in preparation again, she popped up.

The round hit the wall inches from her face, sending shattered stone fragments towards her eyes.

She dropped so fast that Mitch bawled her name, thinking the sniper had got her, but when she hit the ground he saw her legs scrabbling furiously to get her body out of sight. Blood poured down her lacerated right cheek, but she managed to shout a single word.

"NOW!"

Mitch introduced the copper wire to the exposed ports of the battery, muttering a single, breathed word to himself. *Contact.*

Neither of them saw it, but if they had they would have probably enjoyed the sheer level of devastation they had brought upon their enemy.

The vehicle was almost through the choke point, but the rear wheels were only feet away from the rock piles which hid the mines.

As the charge flowed through the buried wires at impossible speeds, the detonators did their one and only job. Both mines exploded simultaneously, vaporising the people advancing between rock face and vehicle. The specially designed v-shaped hull of the Foxhound was powerless to withstand the blast, and with the people walking alongside it so too did the rear wheels disappear as though they had never existed. The back end of the truck concertinaed, violently popping the rear hatch open to crush two men advancing behind it and in what they felt was the safest position.

The advance was stopped dead in a roiling cloud of black smoke like the one which had consumed the gates, only far bigger.

Sabine, far behind with a few others, felt the explosion as the entire world blossomed into fire, smoke and flying debris. The heat from the blast hit her like a shockwave, a snapping sensation like she had received an electric shock, and brought with it deadly fragments of metal and stone. The man to her right jolted and froze before his knees gave way and he fell to the ground, a smoking, twisted scrap of steel protruding from the bloody wound in his face.

"Run," she shouted, turning to see the three surviving men with her had already vanished. Torn between following the others and fearing staying with the others without the protection of Leo. Seeing a rough track up the steep hill to her side, she scrambled upwards and away from sight of the burning wreckage behind her.

Le chasseur was pleased. His bloodlust was beginning to feel slated, and he already relished his victory with anticipation. He was about to be the conqueror, and to the victor would go the spoils.

His momentary daydream was burst, and he flinched despite himself.

The unbelievably loud explosion from the advance below him sent a rush of dust and hot air from ground level all the way up to his position. Leaning over the side and trying to make sense of what had happened below, he watched in disbelief and horror as the dust blew away to reveal his bloodied and broken army lying in ruins below just as the inexorable pull of gravity rained a shower of stone on his position. What went up was now coming down...

His attack had failed, and he was now stranded in the enemy camp. All around him his men looked expectantly for orders, all except the sniper who still stared implacably through his scope.

"This is not over," he told them. "We underestimated our enemy, but if they want us out then it will cost them dearly in blood."

He surveyed the faces looking at him. For the first time since they had sworn to follow his orders, they seemed unsure and afraid. Plans A, B and C were finished, and plan D was simple, vengeful violence.

"WE DO NOT LOSE!" he screamed.

~

Dazed and confused, Simon began to stumble towards the gateway ahead wearing nothing but his underwear. He had two options. Three really, but as he decided staying put wasn't going to help, he faced the choice of back the way he had come from or onwards.

The ground ahead of him erupted in a puff of dust, followed by the echoing report of a rifle.

Slowly, he turned his face to stare upwards at the fort. He saw nothing, but he felt that whoever was up there could see him clearly.

He was past the point of caring if he lived or died; he just wanted the pain to end in either death or sleep. He stared for a few seconds, then turned away and shuffled his bare feet painfully onwards towards the gate. No other shots came.

~

"Did you get one?" came the question to the Legionnaire's right.

"Yes," he lied to the man who wasn't seeing what he was seeing. In his head, he said the words *non-combatant*.

He reminded himself that choosing not to take a shot wasn't the same as missing.

~

Movement near the skyline snatched Claude's attention. The old man had resumed his watch after ensuring that the one man sent to kill him was truly alone.

Now, gently sweeping the barrel of his gun over the terrain he saw a woman scrabbling desperately to gain the high ground away from the place where the explosions had happened. Claude saw her clearly, under no illusion that she was from Sanctuary, and smiled grimly to himself as he settled the crosshairs of his sight on her.

The juxtaposition of old man and state-of-the-art rifle was a thing of beauty as he carefully breathed the rhythm of a marksman which he had done so many times before.

Pausing his breathing at the right moment, he gently squeezed the trigger with a caress of his finger.

The bullet flew true, unwavering in its trajectory. He saw her face as the sound of his shot reached her, fear and shock battling for primacy, too late for her as the projectile travelled at impossible speeds and had already entered her chest.

The impact of the heavy round threw her down like nerveless meat, dead before she hit the ground.

Satisfied that he had acquitted himself well, Claude resumed his scanning of the ground ahead.

STAIRWAY TO HELL

Dan regained consciousness and looked over to see Kate stitching up Mitch's shoulder. He tried to speak but no words came out. He tried again and was rewarded with Kate turning to look at him.

"Hold that," she mouthed to Mitch, handing him the needle and thread she was using. Stepping over to Dan, she mouthed, "Are you ok?"

"Yes," he lied, still in silence.

It was only then he realised that the lack of sound was because of him, not for him.

He was deaf.

"It's probably temporary," Kate mouthed again, meaning his deafness. "You were stood next to an explosion, do you know what happened?"

"Chris," he said, not hearing his own voice so mouthing each word carefully. "Suicide bomb."

His words obviously came out because the others in the room, who hadn't heard the news about who carried the bomb, all stared at him in disbelief.

Mitch, foolishly attempting to carry on with the needle work as he pulled a face to try and see his own shoulder, added to the bad news.

"They're in the fort, too," he said.

Dan didn't see his mouth clearly as he spoke, merely heard a weak noise as though he were underwater, and looked at Kate for a translation.

"He said they are in the fort," she enunciated with deliberate care, this time the pitch of underwater noise changed and Dan could make out some of it; like being able to see shapes in the fog but the hearing version of it.

"How?" he said, rewarding himself with a ringing noise returning to his brain.

Shrugs all round didn't help him, and he sat up despite Kate's protestations. "Anything else?" he asked.

Kate, finally realising what Mitch was trying to do, slapped his hands away and took back control of the stitching. Craning her head back towards Dan she told him, "Everyone is hiding indoors out of sight. People are guarding the gate from the inside and the steps to the fort are barricaded, but we're trapped."

That, Dan understood just fine.

His head ringing and his legs feeling a little unstable, he stood. Kate knew him well enough by now to know that he would not listen to her advice that he should stay in bed for seventy-two hours and rest. She knew that wasn't an option.

He had another infestation to clear; questions and rest could come after.

"There is only one way to do this," Dan said, barely able to hear his own words as he spoke over the tinny whine still ringing in his ears. "We have to climb up and kill them."

His assembled audience was all volunteers, and all understood that without control of the sky fort they were all prisoners under cover of the stone walls. They had no other assets, he told them. They had no way of clearing the fort without going there and doing it themselves. There were no reinforcements and there was no artillery or air support, so they had to do it the medieval way.

He was way past trying to tell Leah she had to stay, he had told her repeatedly all afternoon and into the evening as they planned what they could do.

He wanted to say that this time, of all the times she had put herself on the line, of the times she had saved his life, that this time was different. If their counterattack failed, then he didn't expect anyone to survive. He wanted to say that she had to stay and look after Marie and Ash; that he had to do this for all of them.

From the way he spoke, it sounded as though he had already accepted his death.

Mitch had protested that he had to come, but his wound had debilitated him too much. Dan told him to raise his rifle, and although perplexed at the order, he tried. He tore his stitches and fresh blood seeped through as his face contorted with pain. The wound was simply too big and on a body part which moved too much. He would drop from blood loss before he reached the top of the steps. Dan told him, resolutely, that he had to stay behind.

"And you keep my bloody dog here, too," he finished, brokering no argument on either subject.

Mitch grudgingly accepted that he would be more hindrance than help, and asked what he could do.

"Heal," Dan told him, "and if I fail you starve the bastards out and finish the job."

Dan looked at his assembled volunteers. Neil was there, unwavering in his resolve to protect the town he had grown to love, as were Adam and Pietro and a collection of angry townspeople intent on ridding their home from danger.

He could not fault their commitment or their burning hatred for the men on the mountain who had come to do them harm, but he did doubt their ability on the whole. He kept those doubts to himself.

"Go get some rest," he told them, "and be ready to move in three hours."

Shortly before the sun began to set, before the invaders would have chance to become more entrenched in their position above the town, Dan led the assault. They moved very slowly in the dark, step by step and making sure they reached the top with breath in their lungs. Even to Dan's damaged hearing, the sounds of ragged breathing and the occasional scrape of a weapon on the stone walls sounded impossibly loud in the claustrophobic confines of the near-vertical tunnel they were entombed in.

The climb took close to an hour as they moved slowly, and Dan stopped as the closed door at the top came into view.

The fading light shone around the edges and the air changed almost imperceptibly as they neared the surface. Watching and waiting, he crouched next to Neil who acted as his ears for the interim.

The older man turned to him and shook his head.

No sounds.

Creeping closer as stealthily as he could, he reached the door and peered through a crack in the wood. Nobody guarded the door, instead a large shape had evidently been dragged in front of it to serve as a barricade. Standing carefully, Dan checked all around the edges of the doorframe. He found no wires indicating that it was booby-trapped, nor were any bolts showing in need of blasting away before they attacked. The door was just propped shut.

Glancing back down into the gloom, he saw the faint reflections of eyes staring back at him.

Finding no reason to delay, he braced himself and heaved the door inwards.

—

Leo did not expect an attack up the stairway. In truth, he expected nothing of these weaklings other than to try and flee. His men would pick off anyone foolish enough to show their faces and after that he would accept their imminent surrender. How could they possibly expect to win? He had the high ground, he had destroyed their defences, in part, and he held the advantage.

They were, at the worst possible time, arguing about their position.

This was not something le chasseur was accustomed to, and he did not like it one bit. His orders had always been followed, and nobody had questioned his judgement until that moment.

His men had raised the subject deftly, implying that the tactical situation had changed, so they too should re-evaluate.

They all seemed to want to climb back down the rope and melt away. He stood and stared them all down, burning them with his malevolent gaze. One by one their shame showed and they turned their eyes away.

One man, evidently braver than the others, picked up his weapon and turned his back to walk away.

"Stand still!" Leo snarled. The man paused, but continued without turning.

Drawing the gun from the holster on his waist, Leo told him once more to stay where he was. He didn't.

A single shot sounded, making everyone atop the windswept fort jolt. The man, a bullet lodged in his spine just below his neck, dropped wordlessly. Slowly, deliberately, Leo holstered his sidearm and addressed his men once more.

"Cowards die with bullets in their backs," he said simply.

Just at that moment he heard a noise from the other side of the courtyard.

~

Just after the forlorn hope of attackers had begun to climb the stairs, Leah paced up and down in the hospital with Ash nervously dogging her heels, occasionally emitting a whine of uneasiness.

Mitch, from his enforced position on a bed, grew increasingly frustrated by the girl's inability to stay still.

"You trying to make a bloody trench, girl?" he asked, making her stand still and stare at him.

"What?" she said, half in hostile challenge and partly because she had been too preoccupied to hear his words.

"You're wearing a rut in the stone," he said in a softer tone of voice. She opened her mouth to answer, but a noise to her left down the corridor snatched her attention away.

It wasn't quite a scream, but it was unmistakably a female in distress. Still staring, her open mouth dropped lower as she saw Marie being helped around the corner by Polly.

Her light grey trousers were showing darker all down her legs. Leah's first thought was that she had been shot, seeing as that was popular at the moment, but her brain kicked the information into shape quickly. Mitch saw her face.

"What's happened?" he said seriously, struggling to get up from the bed.

"Marie," she answered woodenly. "The baby's coming."

It was Mitch's turn to stare with his mouth open as the women came through the doorway shouting for Kate.

As Marie was helped back onto a bed and Kate began to fire off a series of professional sounding questions, the soldier turned to the teenager and the two exchanged a look of understanding.

Mitch hated himself at that moment, but he knew he would never even make it up the steps in his condition as he had simply lost too much blood.

He had to leave the task to a child and her pet.

Nodding once, she turned on her heel and stalked away.

Deciding that Mitch didn't really want to be in a room where a woman was going to give birth, he dragged himself out of bed to go and take a seat at the foot of the stairs.

Leah's mind raced as she half walked, half ran through the series of corridors to the barricade at the entrance to the almost vertical tunnel to the clouds.

"Where are you going?" a voice asked her as she pushed past.

"Going to get my dad," she answered.

Dan heard a shot, then burst through the brittle wooden door and into the fading sunlight, weapon raised.

He pressed forward, all semblance of tactics abandoned as he didn't have trained men behind him.

They weren't trained as he was, but everyone spilling out onto the exposed stone was brave and fighting for their lives. Their home.

Neil split off left, just as Dan's peripheral vision clocked the tip of an arrow on his right which led back to one of the most frightening men he had ever seen with his compound bow half drawn.

It struck him that he had never seen the Russian use the bow, but not once did he ever doubt the lethal combination of man and weapon.

No targets were presented, so Dan's training took over subconsciously and he made progress away from the door which would be the obvious point of return fire.

A man rounded the central stone pillar and died with a burst of automatic fire from Dan's HK416.

Two for two, he thought to himself, instantly regretting the fact that his weapon's first kill had been a friend.

Gunfire erupted to his right and he sensed more than saw three of his group drop to the stones. The unfamiliar sound of hissing air, a twang, immediately answered by a butcher's thump of flesh registered in his brain as Pietro neutralised the threat to their right flank. Gunfire to his left made him aware that Neil was in contact, and he pressed onwards.

Speed, aggression, surprise.

He scoffed at himself for using the mantra of special forces; this operation was far from special in any way other than it was a desperate fight for survival. Still, speed was the key. They couldn't have many people on the ramparts of the fort and they had to be cleared away before they had any chance to rally.

The legionnaire sniper heard the stairs door burst open, not taking the time to check what came out. Abandoning his rifle, a thing he had never done, he threw himself into the doorway of the low building which served as the sleeping quarters. Two others followed him, and together they set up a killing ground to cut down anyone who showed themselves. A man with a fair coloured goatee beard leaned around the corner of the stone wall and aimed a rifle, unable to squeeze off a shot before the sniper hit him twice with his backup weapon.

Dan swept onwards, knees bent in his customary crouch, rifle butt pressed into his cheek as his eyes scanned wildly around with the barrel an extension to his vision. Sweeping the gun left and right as he went, the shadows to his right burst into the light.

The gun was shoved painfully into his face, his attacker with one hand on the barrel to prevent it swinging his way. The gun was attached to Dan's vest on the short sling and with the sidearm on his left side he tried to keep control of the rifle with his left hand grasping the angled grip on the barrel. He dropped his right hand from the trigger guard and swept it under his left armpit to withdraw the Walther from its holster, but his attacker had seen the deliberate movement and instinctively knew it was a weapon grab. Finding his right wrist clasped in a vice-like grip, his muscle memory kicked in and he splayed the fingers of that hand out as he turned his wrist to break the grip.

His attacker recognised the feeling of his grip being thwarted and threw his left elbow into the stock of the rifle he held, following the distraction blow up with a change in footing and a knee aimed upwards into the solar plexus.

Dan dropped his body weight, sensing that the kick was coming on a cellular level. The knee connected, but it made a direct hit onto the base of two spare magazines for the assault rifle, prompting an involuntary sharp intake of breath as the pain registered.

The two grappling men slammed heavily into the wall, face to face with an assault rifle between them in disputed ownership. Only then did Dan clearly see the face of the man.

Leo, le chasseur, offended to the very depths of his soul by the gall of this man, this *invader*, snarled in his face.

"I owe you this, Englishman," he growled, just as he brought his head savagely forward into Dan's face.

A crunching noise sounded and hot blood poured over their hands as Dan's nose popped like a water balloon. His eyes stung in sudden, temporary blindness, his ears still rang like a bell and an overwhelming wave of sickness added to the pain as he feared he would drop.

Vomit gurgled in his stomach and threatened to fountain upwards. He felt the pressure on his vest release and, just as Leo had known before, he believed with utter certainty that he withdrew to bring a weapon to bear on him. Releasing the rifle, still blind and on the verge of unconsciousness, he reached for the knife on the front of his left shoulder and whipped it downwards ready to drive it up under the bastard's ribs and put him down.

His shout of rage began to sound as he began his upswing, punctuated terribly by a flash of pain as Leo's knife penetrated deep into his own body, just outside of the protection of the vest.

Dan's knees gave out, and the cry of rage twisted into a strangely muted gasp of unimaginable agony as the weak upward thrust with his own knife merely reached Leo's waist and scored a deep wound. Looking up, Dan saw his own death coming in the form of Leo's hand coming forwards, horribly faster than his own could move, reaching for the grip of the shotgun protruding from over Dan's right shoulder.

Dan saw this. He knew it meant his end; his brutal decapitation by his own weapon.

Just then the sound of claws on stone tapped on his mind, culminating in a snarling, roiling impact of such savage ferocity. His eyes were closed, but he felt the sudden emptiness, felt the concussion of the heavy hit before him as Ash, it could only have been Ash, took the man bodily to the ground a clear three paces from him. The agony he felt intensified as Leo kept hold of the knife and tore it from his body as he was swept away.

His pained relief evaporated when the piercing sound of a yelp of pure agony cut the darkening air like a siren.

NOT LIKE THE MOVIES

Steve stood stock still, eyes closed, waiting for his recurring nightmare to become a reality.

He had achieved his goal. He had freed the population from oppression and he was happy to go into the night now; it saved him from having to face the things he had done and the pain and suffering his master plan had caused.

The shot rang out, but he felt no pain. No violent impact his mind associated with the bullet hitting him, ripping into his flesh, snapping his ligaments and breaking his bones before tearing through his internal organs and leaving him to die in bloody ruin.

The shot sounded loudly. Deafeningly in the close confines of the now crowded town square.

Steve still felt no effect of the shot which he knew would kill him, and he dared to open one eye.

He saw Richards, clutching his left hip just above the bone, and staring in horror at a man on the ground before him.

One of his own men.

Only it wasn't. Benjamin was injured, fatally with three bullets in his abdomen, but his final act was to rid the world of the madman he had tried to overthrow without bloodshed. His plan had cost him his soul, having killed innocent people – something which burned his soul every day and made him wish for it all to end - and worst of all it had now cost him his brother.

The last thing his mother had said to him, her final words, were to look after his little brother, because he always got into trouble when Benjamin wasn't there to watch over him.

Only he had got in trouble, and now he was dead. So was Benjamin's plan to free the people living under fear of capital punishment just to serve the maniac's egotistical vision of the future. He just wanted everyone to get on with their lives, to live together, and dreamed of a day he wouldn't have to do the things he had done before he realised it was all big, fat load of shit. There was no master plan; those who still survived had to work together or they were doomed.

His final act, seconds before he died, was to put all his remaining strength into the trigger of his gun and fire. One bullet, followed by another, followed by a third. His hands held no more blood to work the trigger or hold the gun up any longer.

Benjamin bled out and died; not happy by any possible stretch of the imagination, but feeling like he had accomplished one small thing in his life.

Richards staggered, shocked that he had been shot when he was the one holding the gun. He aimed it at the bastard which he knew, all along, right from the very beginning, was responsible for this ungodly mess. The second bullet hit him in the right thigh, dropping him to the ground and making him kneel at eye height with one of his most trusted soldiers. Questioningly, not understanding the first thing about what had happened that night, he stared into Benjamin's eyes and began to mouth the question, *Why?*

The muzzle flashed a final time and the bullet entered his face just below his left eye, fountaining blood and bone out behind his left ear and ending the year of the Major instantly.

Steve couldn't believe he was alive. Finding Lizzie hugging him tightly, he squeezed her back, kissing her hair, before disentangling himself and taking the steps two at a time in slow motion to stand on the steps.

"Everyone, drop your weapons," he shouted, hands held aloft, as the sounds of metal touching concrete sung out faintly all around him.

"From now on we are all on the same side," he yelled, seeing more confusion than gratitude on the assembled faces of guards and cogs alike.

"What do we do now?" shouted a faceless voice from within the crowd.

The question stumped Steve entirely. He simply hadn't through that far ahead.

He thought for a moment.

"We tidy all this up," he said, waving a hand over the bodies and carnage their revolution had caused, "and tomorrow we start fresh."

FINAL ACT

Leah gained the top of the steps just as she saw Neil fall back clutching his left arm. In the failing light she could already see his face turning pale as he tried to shimmy backwards across the rough stone ground using only his legs.

A noise to her right made her turn and raise her rifle, breathless from the dizzying climb and scared of the bloodbath she had run into.

Ash, the climb showing no evidence of having exhausted him, waited at her left ankle for orders, seeming desperate to get in the fight.

"They're dug in," Neil gasped as Adam dragged him away from danger.

"I will end this!" boomed the accented voice from Leah's right.

Pietro strode past her, thrusting the compound bow and an arrow towards her wordlessly. She took them, without question, and watched as the Russian threw a burning oil lamp onto a pile of bedding.

Gathering up the blankets, seemingly oblivious to the burns he was suffering he stepped around the corner where Neil had just been wounded and threw the blankets though the open aperture of the barrack room. Stepping smartly back untouched by the flurry of shots which answered his sudden appearance, he threw off his prized wolf pelt to escape the flames creeping up his body.

Pietro then fell backwards like a felled tree, landing heavily on the ground Neil had just occupied. Smoke billowed from the room and four men burst out to escape the flames caused by the accelerant.

Leah dropped the bow and raised her rifle, emptying the magazine into the men until they all lay still on the stone, bleeding and twitching. Leah dropped her rifle, still breathless, and ran to Neil's side.

"I'm okay, chicken. Check on Russian Pete," he said through gasps of pain.

Leah nodded and turned away.

She stared into Pietro's glassy eyes, a bullet hole evident on his forehead. The dying sun glinted red and orange from those eyes, making the terrible tragic and beautiful all at once.

A shout made her turn. Picking up the bow she ran to the other side of the ramparts and into view of a sight she dreaded.

A man, as scarred and dangerous as Dan looked, only with a hatred and malevolence she instantly feared, stood over her adoptive father who had been driven to his knees and plunged a knife into him, just as Dan thrust weakly upwards with his own blade.

Ash, needing no instruction and feeling the fear and emotion of the moment more than anyone, threw himself forward, hitting the man with such force as he had never employed before.

Man and dog tumbled end over end and Leah's only reflex was to raise her weapon and kill the man.

Only she wasn't holding her weapon, she held the unfamiliar bow and a single arrow. With an instinct she would never have believed she possessed, she nocked the arrow and drew as far back as her small frame could manage.

The man, terrifying in the failing light, paid her appearance no attention as he drew his hand upwards, spraying blood as he withdrew the blade from Dan's body, kicked the dog brutally and turned ready to drive the knife into Ash.

She drew back, not realising the sheer effort she exerted into pulling the string, and loosed the arrow unthinkingly.

The arrow flew on faith. On instinct. On pure adrenaline.

It hit Leo in the flesh of his left shoulder, and without the strength of the bows original owner it stuck there instead of driving through flesh and sinew to sever the man's spine.

Horrified, in sudden agony, Leo froze. He turned and followed the reverse trajectory of the arrow protruding from his body, to find himself facing a child. A girl.

He hesitated just long enough for Dan to rise, steady his feet, and drive his fist into the neck of le chasseur.

Choking, bleeding from the arrow stuck in his left shoulder and the knife wound in his left flank as well as the chunk of flesh missing from his right forearm from that damned dog, Leo staggered backwards.

The back of his knees hit the low wall at the furthest rampart. One second he was there, the next he was gone; tipped backwards over the wall and into the darkness below.

Leah dropped the bow and ran forward, sliding breathlessly to the stones beside Dan. Ash whimpered tragically to her right but her concentration was focussed solely on stopping the pulsing gouts of blood pumping from the top of Dan's shoulder and rushing through her fingers as she pressed down hard on the wound. His eyes began to roll back as consciousness slipped away.

"Don't you *dare!*" Leah snapped. "You can't go anywhere yet."

Dan's eyes closed.

JUST DESSERTS

He was amazed that he had survived the fall. He was bleeding from half a dozen small wounds from both the plummeting ride from the wall's edge and the fight which preceded it, but finding a soft landing amongst the rock-strewn ground only solidified his narcissistic belief that he was protected by some divine power. It hadn't occurred to him that the soft landing was courtesy of the seven broken bodies he had ordered to be dumped over the walls there.

The hunter would live to fight another day; he would regroup, recruit and return to take this citadel on the coast which had so nearly defeated him. Only the town hadn't beaten him; it had been that damned man and his dog and the girl – *a girl!*

That knowledge stung him the most. Being bested by another skilled man, a hunter not too unlike himself, but for a girl to draw blood from him hurt his pride more than the collection of open wounds and likely fractures which currently made his progress so slow and painful.

In his confusion from the blows to his head and the impact of the earth, he had fled north east, further and deeper into the mountains and away from safety. As the sun sank deeper behind him he penetrated higher into the wild hills where mankind held no dominance in today's world. He was badly hurt, he realised. He couldn't take stock of the blood loss or the mechanical injuries to his back, knee, shoulder and hands. If he could see himself, he would be amazed that he still functioned; but adrenaline and anger alone kept him animated.

Had he been fully alert and capable, he would've first noticed the silent shadows flanking his halting progress from the higher ground long before he did. When his fogged brain finally acknowledged the peril he was in, the terror threatened to rob him of all his remaining strength and resolve. He, *the hunter*, had stumbled straight into an ambush and now suspected he would find lethal enemies on all sides. His only chance of survival now was to find a defensible position and survive the night.

The lead wolf, newly appointed by the process of succession after the death of the previous alpha at the hands of a terrifying Russian, owed his new status to his size and sheer aggression. A vicious and fearless hunter, he had little opposition when he took control of the pack. Now his lips curled back from bright white pronounced canine teeth as he first confronted tonight's meal. He and his pack hadn't eaten for two days, and the emptiness in his belly made his natural savagery that much more razor-edged. He stood squarely in the path of the stumbling creature, widened his stance and issued a blood-curdling snarl with the intention of causing it to take flight. When it ran in fear and panic, they would follow it mercilessly and run it to ground where they would gorge on the warm flesh. The alpha would eat first, forcing every other animal in his diminished pack to wait until he had had his fill before allowing the others to take their turn according to hierarchy.

Seeing the huge grey and black dog blocking his path Leo froze, momentarily terrified that the unkillable bastard and his cursed animal had found him. He knew they hadn't, he was sure he had killed them.

Or had I? he thought.

He could no longer be certain of anything in his pain and fear. Reaching for the weapon holstered on his right hip he froze again, this time in greater fear that the gun he had expected to be there was gone; lost in the fall, probably, and miles behind him. Scrabbling at his pouches and pockets like a deranged smoker searching for a cigarette lighter after a long flight, he found only his torch and a knife to be of any use. More snarls and growls now rippled out all around him as the other wolves tried to startle him into running.

Fire. I need fire, that will scare them away, he thought desperately, only to try the torch in place of flame. The wolves shied away from the bright light which split the night, but only to preserve their vision and not out of any primeval fear as fire would inspire.

For Leo, the fear was far worse.

Instead of the light scaring the animals away it served only to illuminate them in all their savage and beautiful glory. As the torch beam flashed left and right, innumerable pairs of eyes reflected the beam and all were fixed intently on him. Flexing the grip of his weak right hand to better hold the knife, he guessed that he must have broken something in his hand or wrist, as the strength of the grip was far less than he expected to have. How this distracting thought penetrated the smothering blanket of fear was beyond him, and he dragged his thoughts back to the primal need to survive.

Run. Find safety. Hold them off.

He ran, which sealed his fate.

He made good ground at first, moving faster out of terror than he had been before. His initial break gave him confidence, thinking that the wolves would try to hold him there and misunderstanding that their confrontation was designed solely to make him run in panic, to wear himself down to near exhaustion. His elation at breaking free soon evaporated when the snarling and growling shadows rapidly caught up with his shambling progression and kept an effortless pace as they snapped at his heels, herding him easily towards the higher rough ground.

To him, it felt like hours. He ran as fast as he could, stumbling and slipping but the terror and adrenaline rush kept him from losing his footing entirely. To fall would be to die, so he didn't fall. All around him the sounds of excited yapping and barking swum in the night air and added to the horror he was experiencing,

In truth, he ran for less than five minutes before the alpha decided that this particular prey would not require a long chase, and his burning stomach dictated that he sped up the process. Looping in behind him, he checked his pace for a few long strides to match speed and time his bite perfectly. Sinking his elongated canine teeth into the soft flesh just above the knee, the big wolf bit down hard and held on as a shriek of shock and agony tore through the night. The high-pitched squeal of the creature continued as he hit the ground hard, rolling both of them over and over until they came to rest. The wolf had not released the pressure of his bite by one ounce, and still held onto the now mangled and bleeding limb. The thing he had brought down still shrieked, and sat up to raise another limb intent on bringing a shining object down on the wolf's head. Only then did the alpha release his grip and spring forward with an impossible speed brought on by bloodlust and hunger. The shining object dropped from the hand as the wolf's jaw snapped shut on the throat of the creature, instantly stifling the scream and replacing it with a gargling, choked keening noise as the body went rigid.

The fight evaporated and the rest of the pack sidled closer, eager to fill their own empty bellies.

The thing locked into the alpha's jaws spasmed violently, which the wolf took as an act of rebellion. Crunching down harder, and unbeknownst to the animal, one of his canine teeth punctured blood vessels deep into the neck and that release of blood pressure signified the end of the fight.

Bleeding out and partially paralysed from the trauma to his neck, his whole body awash in such unfathomable agony that he couldn't even begin to understand.

Leo's last experience in the cruel world he inhabited, and personally made so much more dangerous, was the sensation of being eaten alive before his heart finally gave out through blood loss. Hunger overtook the rest of the pack, and despite the savage sounds above him as the alpha fought the others away in demonstration of his dominance, the rest of the pack descended to devour him.

The hunter had truly become the hunted.

IT'S A NEW DAY

Steve's declared ceasefire hadn't exactly ended the hostilities of the night. There were more than a few people with scores to settle and the body count had risen slightly.

He found Jan still flat on his back in the arena next to the mangled body of Will, and the two men said nothing. They embraced, tears beginning to flow from the South African's eyes freely. They were not tears of fear or joy, but of remorse, regret, and the sheer chemical force of all the adrenaline leaving his body.

Will, miraculously, survived. He would never walk properly again, nor could he move his neck because of the horrific damage done to him. A life of disability, being cared for by the people he had delighted in hurting, and seemingly lost without his older brother to guide him seemed a more cruel punishment than death.

The vast majority of guards had melted away and now loudly claimed that they felt no allegiance to the regime, merely wanted an easy life. Some of these men and women were given back their guns on good faith, and set to work protecting the camp walls from any possible outside threat instead of acting as jailers.

People followed Steve around, firing questions at him incessantly. He was tired. He ached all over from the exertion of the night and his irritation showed. He turned on one man who had raised a legitimate concern, and spoke more harshly than he intended.

"Who decided I was in charge all of a sudden?" he snapped.

Silence hung in the air as everyone around him glanced left and right hoping someone else would answer. Lizzie rescued the awkwardness of the situation and placed a hand on his shoulder.

"You did," she said quietly, "when you led a rebellion."

Steve had no answer for that. So, he apologised for his tone, explained that he was exhausted, and changed the subject to the burial of the bodies.

Precious fuel was expended as a digger was employed to excavate the earth just outside the camp. Nobody had called for a service as such, but people flocked to the graves as each person was laid inside reverently, regardless of which side they had been fighting for when they fell.

Richards was laid to rest, and whilst a few spat on his grave most people simply seemed happy enough to know that it was over.

Last to go into the ground, his crisp white shirt stained dark with blood, was Max. Steve knelt as the earth was piled in over his body. Patting the dirt softly, he whispered his own silent apology and thanks to the boy.

Life had to go on. They had to eat, they had to grow their crops and tend to their livestock, and they had to rebuild their new way of life. As Steve and his unintentional entourage walked back to the headquarters building, a woman in a semblance of military uniform approached him apprehensively. She stopped in front of Steve, looking as though she wasn't sure whether to salute or not, and cleared her throat.

"Sir," she said hesitantly. "I'm Kershaw."

"It's Steve, not sir," he corrected her as kindly as he could. "And do you have a first name?"

She seemed stunned, but answered anyway.

"It's Anne," she said.

"Hi Anne," Steve replied. "How can I help?"

Anne handed a piece of paper over. "It's from the Americans si—" she said, stopping herself in time. "They want to know our position."

Steve took the paper, seeing a scribbled translation from Morse code to English in note form. Max had mentioned a radio room at one point, but as it hadn't affected their plans at the time he had shelved the thought for later. Now was later.

"Have they given us their position?" he asked her to buy thinking time.

"Yes," she responded simply.

"Do they seem friendly to you, Anne?" he asked.

Surprised at being asked for her opinion on the matter, she gave it some thought, chewing on her lip. She didn't know how best to explain that she could actually tell a lot about an operator from their style of transmission; their nationality, character, even their mood. She knew in seconds from a transmission that one group of survivors were in the Middle East. Deciding not to overcomplicate the answer, she told him, "If I had to guess I'd say yes, they are."

"Then give them our position," Steve said, a thought tickling his mind. "Can you reach everywhere in the world" he asked her.

Anne smiled for the first time. "If they're listening I can."

Steve returned the smile. "Then start broadcasting. Find anyone listening and see who is out there."

A few thousand miles to their south, across the Channel and safely nestled by the sea, an erstwhile paramedic and her veterinarian partner worked hard. They had to multi-task like experts, flicking their attention between a woman in premature labour, a dog with a temper and a large wound on its leg, and two people who had irresponsibly managed to get stabbed and shot.

Muttered complaints about it being all or nothing cut through to Dan's brain, fighting with the high-pitched whine as his hearing slowly returned. He didn't know how he had got back down the steps, or what had happened at the top of the fort.

Vague memories jockeyed for position until one pushed its way to the fore, bringing him back to alertness momentarily. Trying to sit up and being hit simultaneously by the terrible pain on his left shoulder as well as the hand of Sera slapping his head lightly, he lay back down and asked what had happened. Leah appeared over him, dirty and bloodied.

"What…?" he began, until a wave of crippling nausea hit him and he swallowed the next words along with bile. His voice sounded strange, until he remembered his nose had very recently been broken again.

"Relax," she told him, "you're going to need your strength."

His eyes asked the next question, and as Leah looked up towards the doorway to the next room his hearing tuned in enough to hear screams of pain. He couldn't understand why Leah smiled, her bright eyes and white teeth showing from under a mask of dirt and blood. He couldn't form the words, even when the screaming stopped and sounds of sobbing permeated the air. The sobs turned to noises which made him mindful of something happy, before the door opened and one noise sliced the organised chaos in two.

"It's a boy," Kate declared, the sound of Dan and Marie's baby crying in her arms.

"I was right!" Dan said smugly, earning a very teenaged eye-roll from Leah before she left his side to meet her baby brother.

ECHOES

The New Year came and went inside the walls of Sanctuary. Sitting precariously on the parapet above the inky precipice beneath, five people dangled their legs into the abyss and enjoyed a companionable silence.

Behind them, the ravaged ramparts had been cleared but not repaired.

Dan lit another cigarette with difficulty as his left arm was heavily bandaged and in a sling. He tossed the stub of the expired smoke into the small brazier burning behind them, and retrieved his stubby bottle of beer from between his thighs.

Ash rested on the stone walkway close to the fire, his right foreleg also wrapped in bandages, waiting to be needed or entertained. To his left sat Leah, her cheek sporting a half dozen neat stitches, also holding a beer which Dan suspected she might not be enjoying drinking as she barely raised it to her mouth. The furthest left set of dangling legs belonged to Neil, also cradling a small beer bottle which he had emptied quickly and sporting a similar bandage and sling having used the arm to catch two 9mm rounds. Leaning back dangerously he retrieved a second bottle and twisted off the cap with his teeth, took a long pull of it and let out a noise of satisfaction.

The weather was cold but at least it was dry, and blessedly up that high there wasn't a breath of wind for a change. Even though it was dark and the sun had long since set, the moonlight shining a blazing pathway across the ocean looked so picturesque it was difficult to see it and not invoke any emotions.

"What do you miss most?" Neil asked out loud, not specifying who he spoke to or what period of their lives he referred to. Silence hung in the air before Leah fired the first shot.

"Social media," Leah said simply. "What do you *not* miss?" she added, again to the air in general.

"Mess hall food," Mitch interjected sarcastically, his uninjured arm wrapped around Aletta who seemed happy to sit in companionable silence.

"Social media!" said Dan, smirking. "No more wading through adverts to see one mildly funny picture, or being subjected to vague status updates which are clearly just attention seeking shit."

"Sad face emoji," Leah answered with savage mockery and an exaggerated head tilt, picking up the trend of the conversation.

"What's up, hun?" Neil added in an unkind, high-pitched impression depicting a vapid, wannabe socialite.

They chuckled softly, the subject seemingly left open for discussion.

"I miss the internet," Neil added, "although figuring stuff out the old-fashioned way is fun. Sometimes."

"I miss the heating," Leah added, tucking her chin back inside the neck of her thick, black coat. Both men made noises of agreement on that subject.

"I miss driving fast," Dan said wistfully, "not enough smooth road left. No high-octane fuel."

Both Dan and Leah jumped in fright as Neil slapped his thigh, a risky and poorly thought out move given the drop in front of them.

"I just realised something really good," he exclaimed. "How much tax have you paid in the last year?"

It was lost on Leah, not having spent years seeing close to half her income evaporate before her eyes, but Dan chuckled and countered.

"True, but how much have you earned and how many paid sick days did you take?"

Neil made no answer other than a thoughtful grunt. They all knew that their mindless conjecture was filling the empty air to stop their worried minds from wandering too much.

"I miss everyone else," Leah said softly, prompting half a minute of silence as the three of them descended into the grief they had all kept buried deep for so many months.

"Well," she added mischievously, "maybe not *everyone*."

"What do you think happened back home?" Neil said, switching the tempo. "I wish we could talk to them, send them a message or something. We should've brought homing pigeons!"

Suddenly, that thought lurking at the back of Dan's subconscious took form. Gasping, he threw his right leg back over the wall and scissored his left to follow. Abandoning his half-drunk beer on the wall and discarding his cigarette into the flames he walked away to find the annoying man who might know the answer to his as-yet unformed question. Ash sparked into life and followed unquestioningly.

"What was that about?" Neil asked the girl.

"No idea," she answered. "He does that sometimes."

"Like Batman but less cool," Mitch said.

"Debateable," Neil answered, looking back to the moonlit sea and sipping his beer.

Out of breath by the time he had climbed down to ground level and then back up to the tower in the furthest corner of the central keep, Dan finally knocked on the door of Victor's chambers. A heartbeat later he heard, "Oui, entrée," and opened the door.

To his credit, he didn't pull a face or make any comment about having obviously disturbed Victor and Polly in what he suspected was a very private conversation, and scanned the room with his eyes.

"Can I help you, Dan," Victor asked, his embarrassment fading.

"Aha!" Dan exclaimed as his gaze fell on the thing he had seen but not registered every time he had been in the room.

"Does that work?" he said, pointing to an old Ham radio set.

~

Injuries healed. Some scars remained visible where others left no visible sign of the terrible damage suffered. Simon and Lexi made full recoveries, physically, but both seemed hollow sometimes. Paul, despite getting kicked almost to death, was back on his feet inside of a few months but, like the others held by le chasseur, he was never quite the same. Small, comfortable niches were carved out in Sanctuary for them and, mainly out of necessity, life moved on.

Contact was made, with other continents at first, then miraculously with their old family. The news spread fast and became legend told to the next generations. The conversations were slow and difficult, having to use a dog-eared sheet of Q codes and a Morse crib sheet to facilitate the passing of information.

Victor had cleared a wall and marked pins into various parts of the world map, each pin linked by thread to a report on the population and status of other survivor groups. Their discovery about the blood-borne origins of the propagation issue were news to some, but not to all. One group of Americans were neck and neck with a settlement in Canada for the total number of babies born.

It took Dan and his people almost three years to clear every available resource within a possible radius before every drop of fuel was spoiled or spent. After that they used horse-drawn carts but by that time they were self-sufficient with their curious mixture of old and new.

Leah led many of the forays, her own German shepherd cross dogging her heels as she trained it to emulate its father.

They scavenged like they had done at the very beginning, but now their society grew into some amalgamation of medieval technology with some stone-age mechanics thrown in, and mixed into a strange hybrid of renewable energy technology.

They thrived, they grew, and they lived.

They had survived.

AWKWARD CONVERSATION

Thousands of miles apart, two men sat and had the slowest conversations of their lives.

Both had a drink in their hands and smiled at the responses the other gave almost as if they were sharing the moment together.

Dan was speaking, if the unintelligible electronic beeps coming from the radio set could be called that, through an old sailor who had found himself retiring early from the fishing industry as the only surviving person to have experience of Morse code.

Steve, stood over Anne's shoulder as she tapped and listened, spent much of the intervals where their French counterparts were translating explaining the hidden meanings behind their exchanges.

A noise sounded outside the room Dan was in, followed by a shout of his name. Giving his final message to the old man, he finished his drink and went to his duties.

Anne translated the final message for Steve.

"Got to go now, have baby to feed. Stay Safe. D."

EPILOGUE

Stretching her aching back, the old woman rose from her chair and picked up the battered carbine she had carried for years. It was so worn in places that the dappled camouflage pattern she knew every inch of was rubbed down to the smooth metal. Her weapon possessed the last of the working parts for that model, and was as close to its end as she was. She hadn't fired it in nearly ten years, and even then it was to drive away a curious predator, but couldn't quite give up on it. She said she would be buried with it and didn't want it far from her reach; like a Viking warrior wanting to go to Valhalla with her hand gripping a sword's hilt.

Walking slowly, she took the stone steps one at a time until she stepped out onto the exposed walkways and turned to face the bay as her stiff-limbed and tired companion flanked her without instruction. The loyal mongrel hadn't left her side in over a decade; a proud warrior heritage of its great ancestry still present despite the dog's advanced age.

The sinking sun had dropped behind the far cliff and silhouetted the watch tower beautifully, bathing Sanctuary in a rich, golden, fiery glow.

She never got used to how powerful a sunset was. How it stirred feelings in her which reminded her very soul that she was alive.

She had grown sentimental in her old age; prone to reliving stories to an audience who had heard them before but listened out of reverence, respect and entertainment. *The good old days,* she called them, even though there was little that happened during those days which was good. She was permanently wearing her rose-tinted glasses, as was her right having survived for so long through everything the world had thrown at her.

Age did nothing to dull her senses, however, and soft footsteps betrayed the approach of two people. She knew who they were before they got to her, and she was also certain that they were hoping to startle her with their sudden appearance.

Her two nephews, born two years apart and startlingly different in their looks; one tall and broad with a mess of thick, dark hair whilst the other was a head shorter, blonde and smaller in stature with big eyes which seemed to stare straight into a person's soul. Both had the undeniable looks of their grandparents but took more of their personalities from their adoptive aunt.

Between them they held the stewardship of the town now, as she had taken a step back many summers before after twenty years of training them as best she could. Both were effective soldiers, but more than that they were leaders; just like their grandparents. Their joint reign was a return to the times when they at Sanctuary were a warrior clan; a force to be reckoned with.

Before she acknowledged them, something in her subconscious made her turn to the distant watch tower where her parents were buried side by side. She often joked they were buried so close to each other that they could carry on their loving bickering into eternity.

She still missed them, and the pain of their passing lessened only a little each day. She knew they were still watching over their home, buried close to their son who had fallen ill and died not long after they had passed.

She liked to believe that they were still keeping everyone down where she was safe as they had always done, at whatever cost.

"You'll have to be better than that to get the drop on me, boys," she croaked with a smile to herself.

"Still got it, Auntie Leah," said the taller one, leaning in to give her a rough kiss on her cheek which still bore the scar from the battle for Sanctuary.

"I've forgotten more than you know, sunshine," she said with a grin, goading them both into a good-natured argument for her amusement.

"Always," said the shorter one, deftly and diplomatically avoiding the bickering she tried to antagonise as he bent to scratch under the chin of the German shepherd cross who looked up at him expectantly. Producing a scrap of dried meat, he rewarded Ash's descendant as she knew he would.

"All quiet," said Jack before the woman cut him off.

"You don't need to tell me," she said. "I'm retired."

Her nephews exchanged a look, which she somehow detected even though she still gazed out over the ramparts.

"And don't roll your eyes at me," she said before turning to face them. She knew they didn't want to report anything to her; they wanted advice on something whist they could still call on her experience.

"What can an old woman do for you?" she enquired with sweet sarcasm.

"Nothing," said Peter, the shadow of the old compound bow jutting out above his shoulder, "we just wanted to see how you were."

"I'm fine," she said, "in fact I was just about to go and visit my granddaughter."

Jack smiled back at her before saying, "We'll walk with you, Auntie Leah."

A little over a week later, over a hundred men and women of all ages made the long and arduous journey on foot to the top of the cliff overlooking their beautiful home.

They lowered her shrouded body into the rectangular hole as her daughter knelt in the dirt to reverently lay the battered and ancient gun on her chest. Her body was almost covered by the time everyone had filed past and sprinkled a handful of dirt over her, leaving her nephews little work to do in replacing the remainder of the excavated soil. Her granddaughter was the last to stand over her with her uncles; fourteen years old and strong, with a fierce sense of pride in her heritage, she was the very image of the woman they laid to rest. In reverent flattery of her grandmother, she carried with her an old rifle everywhere she went. The short barrel with its angular foregrip. The dual sight on the top rail. It had belonged, originally, to a man now immortalised in the legend of her home. A man she had never met but felt like she knew nonetheless.

Carefully arranging the stone slab to align with the others, they gently patted down the earth to tuck her in tight, next to Dan.

She was in fine company on that ridge. The vanguard of warriors who fought their whole lives to protect the group, never once giving up or putting their own needs ahead of others. Those responsible for the safety they now enjoyed.

She lay beside her Uncle Neil. Mitch beside him.

The best friend of her childhood, Ash.

She lay beside her younger brother, taken too soon.

She lay behind the woman who had become her mother, and a mother to so many others.

She lay beside the man who started this wild ride she called her life. The man who had brought them all together and had become her father. A man who almost died so many times to keep them safe. A man she loved. A man she admired.

A man she was certain she would see again when they were reunited.

This was Leah's final resting place. She had survived, she had retained her humanity throughout countless ordeals, she had grown into a society she had led with fairness and tenacity for many years. She had lived with hope in her heart, found sanctuary and above all else had endured when events had so many times conspired to finish her.

That was Leah's rebellion.

The end of the AFTER IT HAPPENED series

A message from the author

This series has meant so much to me; more than I can even begin to explain. It began as a dream, became an obsession, was filed away and ridiculed as a hobby and in the end, became a life-changing choice.

The journey that Dan *et al.* have taken me on is deep and meaningful in so many ways which I won't bore you with, instead I want to thank you – my readers – for bringing this whole thing to life. If you hadn't have taken a chance on this, if you hadn't liked it and caused that snowball to roll downhill and gather momentum then it's highly unlikely that the events after the characters' lives at the prison would ever have been written, and those characters you have come to know would have been saved from the suffering and torment I put them through.

And they wouldn't have found peace in their safety to live out their lives. It would've just *Happened*, and there would have been no *After*.

We all have walls to hide behind in our lives, and stepping outside of your own personal Sanctuary to bring the fight to the enemy takes bravery, in whatever small way it begins. Step outside of your comfort zone, do something selfless, take the hit and recover to fight again. We learn only when we make a mistake.

This is by no means an announcement of my retirement, far from it in fact as by the time you read this I will have already started or likely published the first book of my new series. I hope you're ready to leave behind post-pandemic Europe and travel further in time with me to an alternative dystopian future, because that's where I'm headed right now.

I say this often, but not often enough.

Thank you.

Keep Reading.

DCF

Facebook: @devonfordofficial

Twitter: @DevonFordAuthor

www.devoncford.com

It doesn't end there…

In a world where there are no rules, there is no greater hero than a seventeen-year-old girl.

Life at the fortified town of Sanctuary is calm. The people, with their fearless leader at the helm, have created a haven where they can live out their lives in peace and safety.

But it hasn't always been this way. There were battles and losses along the way, and victory usually came at a price.

With the younger generation coming into their own, it's time for Leah to pass on all she has learnt over the years. Time to tell the stories of how the world became the way it is…starting with the **highwaymen of Andorra.**

CPSIA information can be obtained
at www.ICGtesting.com
Printed in the USA
BVHW031958120323
660268BV00016B/239